LOVE'S SWEET SURRENDER

SHERYL LISTER

ABOUT LOVE'S SWEET SURRENDER

The moment divorcée Maxine Richardson crosses paths with Christian Davis, sparks fly in more ways than one. She's stunned by the intense attraction between her and the aggravating man, and is determined to fight it, even if he is fine as wine. However, beneath his gruff exterior is a man whose kiss awakens Max's deepest desires and entices her with a passion she can't resist.

For years, Christian has guarded himself against love and the heartbreak that always seems to follow. But Max, with her voluptuous curves and sexy smile, ignites a fire inside him he never sees coming. She's knocking down his walls with each sensual encounter and tempting him with the promise of forever...if he would only surrender.

For all of you who patiently waited for Max's story.

ACKNOWLEDGMENTS

My Heavenly Father, thank you for my life and for loving me better than I can love myself.

To my husband, Lance, you will always be my #1 hero!

To my children, family and friends, thank you for your continued support. I appreciate and love you!

To my writing tribe, thank you for being you.

A very special thank you to CHP Officer Chris Miller for sharing your expertise.

To all my readers, thank you for your support and encouragement. I couldn't do this without you!

CHAPTER 1

*M*axine Richardson adjusted the large tote bag filled with a variety of toys on her shoulder, made her way up the walkway and rang the doorbell. "Hi, Natalie," she said, smiling at the woman who opened the door.

Natalie brought a hand to her mouth and held the door opened. "Oh, Maxine, I'm so sorry I forgot call you."

The woman's red puffy eyes sent a frisson of fear down Max's spine. She stepped inside. "What's going on?"

"Lilah passed away last night. It was the seizures."

She laid a comforting hand on Natalie's arm. "I am so sorry. Is there anything I can do?" Max loved her job as a pediatric occupational therapist, but she'd never gotten used to losing one of her babies. She'd been seeing eighteen-month-old Lilah weekly for almost a year and the little girl had suffered from epileptic seizures that the doctors had been trying—with little success—to control.

"I don't think so. I...um...I should cancel her other therapy appointments." The tears started again.

"I can do that." Her friend and colleague, Caroline

Matthews, was Lilah's physical therapist and Max would call her as soon as she got back in the car.

Natalie gripped Max's hand. "Thank you so much for everything you did for Lilah. Even though she wasn't alert a lot of the time, she always smiled when she heard your voice."

Max could feel her emotions bubbling up. *I am not going to cry.* "Thank you for saying that. You know I loved your little princess." She gave Natalie a strong hug. "Please let me know if you need me to do anything."

She nodded. "I'll let you know when we make the arrange —" Her lips trembled and fresh tears ran down her cheeks. Another woman came from the back. "This is my mother," Natalie whispered.

Max introduced herself, offered condolences and left the women to their grief. As soon as she was back in her car, she felt the sting of her own tears. When she made the decision to specialize in pediatrics twenty-seven years ago, particularly the birth to three population, she knew she'd have little ones with physical and developmental disabilities that ranged from minor to severe. Unlike some of the therapists she'd worked with over the years who had no difficulties remaining detached, Max formed bonds with the babies almost instantly. Because she was in the home weekly, many parents thought of her as a favorite aunt of sorts and losing one of her precious ones felt as though she'd lost a family member.

Bringing her emotions under control, she made the call to Caroline, then cranked up her music. She needed a lift. Since she had a few extra minutes, Max decided to stop and pick up a few supplies. Instead of taking her usual route, she detoured through the neighborhood. She hadn't gone six blocks when she heard the siren behind her.

"What now?" she muttered. Max hadn't been speeding

and she didn't know any other reason why she was being stopped. Pulling over to the curb, she waited for the officer to appear. Out of her side mirror she could see the officer approaching—dark golden brown skin, tall, good-looking.

"Good afternoon. License and registration please. Are you aware that you just ran a stop sign?"

"I didn't see a stop sign." She took the registration from her glove compartment, then pulled out her favorite Black Panther wallet and retrieved her driver's license. She handed them to the officer. Max glanced in her rearview mirror and spotted the sign that had been hidden by an overgrown tree. "The sign is covered by the trees and there's nothing painted on the street." Sighing inwardly, she wished she could start the day over.

He checked both her documents and handed them back. "The city is supposed to take care of it. Just be careful."

Grateful that he didn't plan to give her a ticket, she relaxed. "Thank you, and I will."

He nodded and strolled back to his car.

Max made a quick stop at the store and, by the time she arrived at her next client's home, she was back in control and figured her day could only get better. It turned out to be short-lived, however, because halfway through the session with two-year-old, Aiden, his mother burst into tears in response to Max's question about how the previous week had gone with the suggested activities.

"The physical therapist was yelling at me because she said I hadn't stretched Aiden enough." Aiden had been diagnosed with spastic cerebral palsy and his leg and arm muscles tended to be tight, which interfered with his mobility and upper body function. "I tried to do it, but I had to help my other son with his homework, cook and clean, and sometimes, I just want to take the boys for a walk or go to the park. I just want to be the mom, not a therapist," she cried.

It is only Monday. "You're right, Bonnie. You are Aiden's mom and it's our job to be the therapists." Aiden's physical therapy was provided by another company. Max had met Latrice Irvin and found the woman had little compassion for the families, tended to be a know-it-all and acted as if the only goals that mattered were the ones *she* wanted. They'd butted heads before when the woman had tried to tell Max how to do her job. Latrice found out quickly to stay in her lane.

Bonnie handed Max a sheet of paper that had a long list of exercises and activities the PT had assigned that were supposed to be done four times a day. Max could see why Bonnie was frustrated. Even Max wouldn't be able to keep that schedule and she lived alone.

"I don't know what to do."

"I can show you a few ways to incorporate some of the activities into your day that will hopefully give you a little breathing room." Max knew her session might run over if she took the extra time needed, but she'd never left a parent in need and wouldn't start today. "Can you excuse me for a moment so I can make a phone call?"

"Of course."

Max grabbed her cell out of the tote, along with her appointment book and dialed the number to her last client. She typically scheduled new evaluations at the end of the day because they often ran longer than an hour and she hoped the mom would be okay with the slight delay. After quickly explaining the situation, the woman graciously expressed her understanding and told Max not to rush or worry. Returning her phone and book to the tote, she smiled at Bonnie and proceeded to share some tips. "How many times a day do you change Aiden's diaper?"

Bonnie let out a snort. "At least seven or eight times."

"Then maybe you can incorporate some of the leg

stretches during that time." She demonstrated and had Bonnie repeat the exercises.

"Oh, my goodness. That was easy."

"Yes. You can also make it a game during dressing or bathing...like smelling his feet and gently stretching to let him do the same. Now as far as going for a walk, that's the perfect time to work on reaching. There are a number of flowers and leafy trees and bushes on your street. Point out the flowers, their colors and texture and have him try to reach for them. I'd carry a small package of hand wipes to clean his hands right after, since he still likes putting his hands in his mouth."

"Max, you have no idea how much you've helped me. I don't know how to thank you," Bonnie said emotionally. "When I asked the other therapist, she made me feel like a bad mom for not doing everything on her list."

Max gave her a gentle smile. "You're a wonderful mother, and Aiden is making good progress toward his goals." She picked up the toddler and he immediately reached for her lips. "Yep, you're doing well with the reaching, aren't you?"

Aiden giggled and babbled something.

She handed him to Bonnie. "I need to get going."

"So do I. I almost forgot I need to pick up Mark from school."

Max smiled. It was mid-September and most districts had been in school for almost a month. Even though the season would change in a week to fall, the ninety-degree weather didn't care.

"Thank you again for taking this extra time. I know you didn't have to, and I appreciate it. Please pass along my apologies to your next client."

"You're very welcome." Max packed up all the toys and stood. "I'll see you next week." She hustled out to her car, dumped the toys into the bin she had for the dirty ones and climbed in behind the wheel. She used the hand sanitizer she always kept available, then programmed in the next address to her GPS. Thankfully, the next stop was only fifteen-minutes away and less than ten minutes from her own house.

While driving, Max mentally went over the nine-month-old little girl's history, so she'd know what equipment she needed for the assessment. Once she arrived, she quickly gathered everything, rushed up the walkway and rang the bell. She went still upon seeing the man who opened the door. He was the same CHP officer who had pulled her over earlier. "Hello, I'm Maxine Richardson, the occupational therapist. I have an appointment for Malia's assessment. I apologize for—"

The man glared at her. "It's about time. Are you always forty-five minutes late for your appointments?"

So much for him being a nice guy. "With all due respect, Mr. Jones, I called your wife to let her know I'd be late and she indicated she didn't have a problem. I had a slight emergency with my previous client and I hope you'll be as under-standing as your wife. I would do the same for your daughter should the need arise." Max congratulated herself on keeping her smile in place and her voice calm and even, when she really wanted to toss professionalism to the side and tell this irritating man about himself. He opened his mouth to say something, but a woman holding a baby approached. His wife, Max assumed.

"Christian!" She glared at him, then turned Max's way with a smile. "I'm so sorry, Ms. Richardson." She hipped the man aside and opened the screen. "Please come in. I hope everything is okay with your client."

"Yes, it is. Thank you."

"I'm Sandra and this is Malia," she said, smiling at the baby cradled in her arms. Her smiled faded. "You've already met my brother, Christian. Come on back."

Brother? "Nice to meet you all," she said, following the woman through a spacious tri-level home to an even larger family room with leather furniture, fireplace and huge entertainment center holding a flat-screen TV. Max could feel the heat of Christian's stare on her back, but she didn't turn around or acknowledge him. After the day she'd had, one more thing just might push her over the edge.

Christian Davis took up a position against the kitchen bar that connected to his family room, folded his arms across his chest and observed the therapist settle on the loveseat. He didn't know what he expected—maybe another brusque, pinch-faced therapist like the last three—but it wasn't this beautiful goddess with skin the color of whipped mocha and enough voluptuous curves to stop traffic for days. It took him a moment to realize that she was the same woman he'd stopped for running a hidden stop sign earlier. She'd shocked him, though. At the door, she'd read him up one way and down another, all without raising her voice and with a smile that had hit him straight in the gut. He tuned in to the conversation as his sister shared Malia's medical history and felt his anger rise. Chris blamed Sandra's jackass ex-husband's abusive behavior for his niece being born three months prematurely.

"Can you tell me some of the things Malia is doing—grasping, reaching, keeping her head up?" Max asked.

"She closes her fingers around mine," Sandra said. "But she's not doing any of those other things. I don't really know what to do and all the other therapists said..." She trailed off and swiped a tear from her cheek.

Chris' heart clenched. The previous three therapists had all but told his sister not to get her hopes up where Malia was concerned. Each time, it broke his sister's heart a little more, thereby breaking his, too. He wouldn't stand for another one to do it again. He took the few steps into the family room. "If you're planning to tell us there's nothing you can do or that we should just make her *comfortable*, you can just pack up now and not waste our time."

Maxine slowly turned his way and angled her head. "Mr. um—"

"Davis," he said.

"Mr. Davis, I can't tell you one way or another developmentally what your niece will or won't be able to do in the future. What I can say is that I'll evaluate her current skill level and if therapy is indicated, we will determine some appropriate short and long-term goals."

"Can you excuse us for a minute, Ms. Richardson?" Sandra said, placing Malia in her carrier and standing.

"Please call me Maxine or Max, and of course."

His sister marched over to where he stood, latched on to his arm and nearly dragged him down the hallway toward the bedrooms.

"What is *wrong* with you, Chris?" Sandra whispered harshly. "Maxine is the first therapist who has shown the slightest interest in helping my baby and you're going to mess it up."

"I'm just making sure she doesn't turn out to be like the last few."

She poked him in the chest. "No, you're being a pain in the ass. Don't you have somewhere to go? You can come back in an hour, *after* she's gone."

Chris chuckled. "Are you throwing my out of my own house?"

"If that's what it takes, *yes*," she answered through clenched teeth.

He studied his sister. She was pretty angry with him.

Thirteen years her senior, he was very protective of her and did everything in his power to make sure she had what she needed. That was why he'd opened up his home to Sandra six months ago when she had finally decided to leave her husband. He sighed. "Fine. I'll back off. For now."

Sandra smiled, leaned up and kissed his cheek. "Thank you. I have a good feeling about her." She started back down the hall, then paused. "If you're coming back, promise you'll behave."

One part of him said he should probably leave, but the other part of him couldn't do it. Sure, he wanted to make sure the woman did what she came to do, but he also admitted to himself that part of his anger had to do with the fact that he'd been instantly attracted to the therapist. Something he couldn't remember happening with a woman since…never. "Okay." Chris blew out a long breath and followed her back to the family room. He stopped short upon seeing Maxine sitting on the floor in front of the carrier holding a toy and talking to Malia. Whatever she'd said had his niece smiling and laughing. The sound warmed his heart.

Sandra passed him on her way back to the sofa and gave him a smug smile. "I told you."

He was grudgingly impressed as he watched Maxine engage Malia and ask Sandra detailed questions. He went to the kitchen and grabbed a bottle of water. *Maybe it would be different this time.* None of the others had stayed longer than five minutes, but Maxine Richardson didn't waste time trying to get to know Malia. Chris twisted off the cap and took a long drink. He turned and choked. Max was lying on her stomach in front of his niece, who was now in the same position on the floor. The sight of her wide hips, curvaceous ass and thick thighs in the black stretch crop pants nearly stopped his heart and sent a jolt of lust straight to his groin.

Coughing, he tried to catch his breath. At forty-nine, he couldn't remember the last time he'd reacted to a woman so strongly. And he was way too old to be starting now.

As if sensing the reason for his plight, his sister smiled his way and asked sweetly, "Are you okay, Chris?"

Still trying to force air into his lungs, he nodded. "Fine," he croaked. "Just went down the wrong pipe."

Maxine glanced over her shoulder and viewed him with concern. "Are you sure you're okay?"

I will be as soon as I stop fantasizing about running my hands all over your body. The thought shocked him further and brought on another coughing fit. He cleared his throat several times and took a careful sip of water. Thankfully, without any issues. "See, fine." His eyes locked on Max's for a lengthy moment and he felt another jolt. "I'm good." Chris slid onto one of the barstools and shifted his body away from both women so they wouldn't see just how much he'd been affected. He scrubbed a hand across his forehead. What was his problem? He was damn near *fifty*, but his body had reacted as if he were half that age.

It took a minute for his body to calm down before he could focus his attention on the activities going on in his family room. This time, Max had his niece sitting on the floor between Max's legs. Chris watched in fascination as Malia attempted to hit a switch after Max had demonstrated it a few times. Though the little girl's hand only moved a few inches, she seemingly understood what was needed to make the toy light up. Once again, emotion clogged his throat. He caught Sandra's gaze and knew she felt the same hope he did. By the time Max had packed up and left, Chris agreed with his sister—Max was different. Very different.

"Well?" Sandra asked after she came back from seeing Max out.

"She's good."

"She's really good. Did you see how Malia responded to her? For the first time, I think my baby is going to be okay." She glanced over at the baby asleep in the carrier. "I don't know if she'll ever catch up and be normal like other kids, but—"

Chris wrapped his arm around her shoulder and kissed her temple. "Hey, we're not giving up hope. Malia will be Malia and we're going to do whatever is necessary to make sure she can reach whatever level she can."

Sandra buried her head in his chest. "I don't know what I'd do without you. You're the only one who's always been there for me. Mom called yesterday and said she couldn't see why I was wasting my time and hadn't put Malia in foster care, so I can live my life."

His anger rose. Their mother hadn't been a model parent —neither had their father for that matter—and was the last person who should be doling out any advice about raising children. "I hope you ignored her."

"I did." She stepped out of his embrace. "She already knows how I feel and I told her not to bring it up again." Sandra folded up the blanket that had been on the floor. "You know, you owe Max an apology," she said casually.

He groaned inwardly at how he'd acted initially. "You're right. I'll make a point of being here when she comes next time and apologize."

She smiled. "She'll be here Tuesday two weeks from now at three. I made sure to schedule the appointment at that time so you'd be off work."

Chris' workday ended at two-thirty and he would defi- nitely be home in time for the session. He shook his head, but couldn't suppress his smile. "I guess you're going to make sure I get it done, sooner rather than later."

Sandra nodded. "Yep. And you should probably make it a

really good one because I can tell you like her. As in you're attracted to her," she added pointedly.

Chris lifted a brow. "What makes you think that?"

"The little choking incident." She waved a hand. "And don't bother to deny it. I saw the way you were looking at her."

What could he say? His sister knew him well. Yeah, his apology needed to be better than good because for the first time in a long while he wanted to get to know a woman.

CHAPTER 2

*S*aturday afternoon, Max rang her friend, Nzinga Carlyle-Walker's doorbell.

"Come on in, Max."

Max hugged Nzinga and stepped inside her friend's new home. "Marriage looks good on you, girlfriend, and that smile says the honeymoon was all that and more."

Nzinga laughed. "It was." The pediatrician had reconnected with her childhood crush at their high school reunion the past June and had married three months later. They'd just returned from their honeymoon in the Bahamas.

She glanced around the spacious and elegantly decorated house. "I love this."

"So do I. What made it even better was only having to move everything less than two miles. I didn't even box up the clothes. Just took them from the old closet to the new one."

"That's what I'm talking about." Max and Nzinga, both, lived in Roseville and only a few miles apart. "Donna and Val here yet?" Donna Harper and Valina Anderson rounded out the quartet of friends who had been together since sixth grade. The four of them made a practice of getting together at least once a month and rotated homes. Because Nzinga and her new husband, Byron, had just purchased the new house, Nzinga had volunteered to host.

"No, you're the first," Nzinga called over her shoulder as they walked through the kitchen to an enclosed sunroom similar to the one she'd had in her previous home.

Max dug a small gift-wrapped box out of her tote. "I got you a little house-warming gift."

"Girl, you didn't need to buy anything." Nzinga carefully removed the paper and opened the box. She burst out laughing. "I don't know about you, Max."

She grinned. "Byron will thank me." She'd purchased sexy lingerie. "Speaking of Byron, where is he?"

"Right here," Byron said, entering the sunroom. "How are you, Max?" He leaned down and kissed her cheek.

"Good. You've been wearing that same smile since the class reunion. I like it." He happened to be in town visiting his younger brother, who was in Max and Nzinga's graduating class and attended the family picnic. Because Byron had been three years older, Nzinga's parents had forbidden their relationship at the time. However, both sets of parents were ecstatic that the two had reconnected and married.

He placed a kiss on Nzinga's lips. "Hey, what can I say? My baby keeps me smiling." He glanced down at the silky material in the box. "What's this?"

"Oh, a little housewarming gift," Max said with a wink.

Byron wiggled his eyebrows at his wife. "I think I'm really going to enjoy this gift."

Nzinga swatted him on the arm, but her smile was still in place. "Aren't you leaving?"

"Yep. Don't want to be involved in all the gossip that's going to be flowing in here once the rest of the Sassy Seasoned Sisters get here," he said with a laugh. The moniker had been given to them by Donna's daughter and she'd made

T-shirts that the four friends had worn to the class reunion picnic the past summer.

"Bye." She pushed him out of the room.

Max smiled. "Y'all are so cute together." For a brief moment, she envied their private smiles, gentle kisses and soft caresses. She couldn't remember the last time a man had looked at her the way Byron did Nzinga. And as far as kisses went, the few she'd shared with men she dated since her divorce six years ago weren't worth remembering.

Nzinga slid the box top back in place and set it on a small side table. "I never thought I could be this happy."

"You've earned it after wasting over two decades with that asshole, Melvin." She had never cared for Nzinga's ex-husband. He always walked around with a holier-than-thou attitude and talked to Max, Val and Donna as if they were the hired help.

Nzinga chuckled. "Speaking of no-good exes, how are things going with Dion?"

Max shrugged. "Nothing's changed much. Whenever I call to check on him, the conversations are awkward and barely last more than a minute or two. Then again, I guess that's progress, since six months ago, our only communication was by text." She had been estranged from her twenty-three-year-old son, Dion, since divorcing his father six years ago. Max's ex had cheated on her and spun it to insinuate that she had been the one. Dion had taken his father's side and, outside of telling her son that she had been faithful to his father, she had chosen not to give the then seventeen-year-old the proof she had of his father's infidelity. "Sometimes, I wonder if I should've just told him what his trifling father had done, especially after the smug looks he kept giving me at Dion's graduation." After the ceremony, Max had tried to take pictures, but her ex kept finding ways to pull their son away to meet one person after another that he'd invited.

Giving Max a quick hug, she said, "I believe everything is going to work out and Rolando is going to get his, just like Melvin." The ex-city councilman's bid for governor had ended abruptly after his multiple affairs and out of wedlock son—who had been conceived during his marriage to Nzinga—came to light. The man had all but faded from the spotlight.

"I just hope I'm around to see it." The doorbell rang.

"Be right back."

Nzinga came back a moment later with Donna and Val. After a round of hugs and greetings, she took them on a tour of the new house.

"This is gorgeous," Val said. "And that backyard is the perfect entertainment spot."

"With both our families here, we thought the same. Byron has already decided to have a barbeque next weekend for everybody." Nzinga led them back to the kitchen. "I figured I'd go old school for lunch today—fried chicken, potato salad, baked beans and homemade rolls."

Donna shook her head. "It's a good thing I work out because I'm about to hurt myself." The former police officer and Army veteran still kept up with her exercise regimen.

They all burst out laughing and Max said, "I'm going to need to get on your program, girl, because I plan to hurt myself, too." She fully embraced her five-eight, size sixteen curves, but she still wanted them to be tight and tried to work out at least three days a week.

Donna held up a gift bag. "Well, before we all hurt ourselves with all this good food, I have something for y'all from Monique." Her twenty-six-year-old daughter and goddaughter to the other three women, always made a point of giving them small gifts. She handed each one a black stainless steel travel cup with *Sassy Seasoned Sisters* engraved on the outside. It even had a picture of a fly woman wearing sunglasses, that personified the term *sassy*. Over the summer, the younger woman had also had T-shirts made with the same phrase that they'd all worn to the class reunion.

"Aw, I love my goddaughter," Max said, turning the cup one way and then another. "And it's huge. This thirty ounces will keep me from having to stop to buy water halfway through my day. Tell her thank you."

Nzinga and Valina echoed similar sentiments, then they all carried the food out to Nzinga's sunroom.

Nzinga went to the kitchen and came back with a pitcher. "I made some iced tea…with a little something extra."

"Alright now." Donna poured herself a glass and took a sip. "Now *this* is what I'm talking about."

Once settled around the table, lively conversation ensued as they filled their plates and caught up on each other's lives. Max always looked forward to hanging out with her girls. She bit into a warm drumstick and moaned. "Girl, you outdid yourself with this chicken."

Nzinga chuckled. "Byron said the same thing and snagged three pieces before he left."

"I don't blame him," Val said, scooping up a forkful of potato salad. "I think we should just crown you the queen of the kitchen and pay you to make all the food for our get-togethers."

She waved Val off. "I don't think so. All of you cook just as well as I do." They laughed. "Anyway, what's up with this dinner and dance the reunion committee is throwing the first weekend in November? I just got the invitation yesterday."

"Ever since the band played at the reunion, people have been asking about us doing something, so we came up with that idea. We'll play for half the evening and have a DJ for the other half. Me and my drums have been practicing non-stop."

Max lifted her glass in a mock toast. "I can't wait." Their high school jazz band had rocked the house during the reunion. The conversation turned to how the week went. Max took a long sip of her spiked tea. "I really needed this after my crazy week. I started my Monday losing one of my babies."

"Oh, no." Nzinga placed a comforting hand on Max's arm. "I know how attached you get to your babies."

"Yeah." Even now, the thought made her chest tighten with emotion. "Then I got stopped by a CHP officer for running a stop sign that I didn't see because it was hidden behind an overgrown tree."

"What?" Donna said. "I know that cop didn't give you a ticket. You want me to investigate his behind?" The former Army veteran and police officer owned a private investigation firm.

"No, he didn't." She thought back to the encounter and how nice he'd seemed initially, then got mad all over again when she recalled his later behavior.

"Ah, what's up with that expression?" Val asked with a grin. She leaned forward. "Exactly what did this officer look like?"

"Tall, fine, dark golden brown almost bronze-skinned with hazel eyes and a nice body, but—"

"Dang, girl, there's more?"

Max nodded. "Yep. I ran into him later that day at a client's house and he was rude as hell." She told them about being late and why, and how understanding the client's mother had been. "It took everything I had not to cuss him out, especially after the day I'd had."

Nzinga shook her head. "What did his wife say?"

"Nothing. She's his *sister*." They all stared at her, smiling. "What? Wait. I know y'all aren't thinking—."

Donna nodded slowly. "That's exactly what we're thinking."

"Okay, just no." She waved a dismissive hand. "You must be out of your mind, Donna."

"I don't think so, and you know why?"

Max took a sip of her tea. "I'm not really interested, but I'm sure that's not going to stop you."

Donna smiled. "Nope, it's not." She propped her elbows on the table and rested her chin on her clasped hands. "Even though you were mad as hell, you still managed to study the brother long enough to give a better description of him than some of my clients."

Nzinga nodded. "And did you hear how her voice changed when she said it?"

"What?" Max divided her gaze between the three women wearing wide grins. "I think y'all need to lay off this spiked tea because you're hearing things."

"Mmm hmm. Oh, and I should probably warn you, girl, those eyes will get you every time. Mark my words. I should know."

She understood exactly what Nzinga meant. Every girl in their high school had been mesmerized by Byron's light brown eyes. However, Max didn't plan to be mesmerized by anything except the therapy services she'd be providing to his niece.

Val gestured Max's way with her glass. "Exactly. So after he apologizes—and I know he will—you can invite him to the dinner and dance."

She reached over and plucked the glass out of Val's hand. "You've definitely had enough." They all burst out laughing. Yes, the man was good-looking, but the only place Max wanted to take Christian Davis was to the edge of a cliff and drop him off.

Chris stared at the cards in his hands and wished he'd declined his friend's invitation. The woman seated next to him had plastered herself against his side from the moment he had arrived at the Saturday evening gathering and Chris hadn't been able to shake her no matter how hard he tried. He leaned forward to throw out a card and, in the same motion, shifted slightly to create some space between him and the woman with her cloying perfume.

"Chris, I'm glad you're my partner," his friend Matthew Harris said as he slammed a card down and collected the book. "We're gonna wipe the floor with you clowns," he added with a laugh.

Matt divided an amused glance between Chris and the woman and Chris shot him a dark glare. Over the past few months, Matt and his wife, Leila, had taken it upon themselves to fix him up with one woman after another. Leila had claimed that she was concerned about Chris growing old alone. Chris had pointed out he liked his life just fine. Sure, loneliness reared its ugly head from time to time, but he couldn't see himself expending the necessary energy it took to establish a relationship. He'd been there and done that before and come away with his heart in shreds. No, he had no desire to revisit those emotions again. He preferred to date when it suited him and the woman at his side—Nichelle something or other—wouldn't make the list even if he'd been looking. While Chris was all for a confident and assertive woman, one who all but propositioned him five minutes after the introduction was a hard pass. Instantly, an image of Maxine and her curvy body floated through his mind and he wondered which category she fell into. He shook himself and tossed out another card.

"Man, y'all are killing us," a man from the losing team groused.

They finished the hand and Chris stood. "Somebody else can take my place. I'm going to get something to drink."

Nichelle jumped up. "Oh, I'll get it for you, Chris. Just tell me what you—" she added with a wide smile.

"No," he said, cutting her off. "I mean, I can get it. Why don't you take my place?"

Matt chuckled. "I could use another partner since I'm not ready to relinquish my throne as King of Spades." Everyone around the table groaned.

Nichelle glanced Chris' way, then at the table. Finally, she slid into the chair. "I guess I can play a hand or two."

Releasing the breath he didn't realize he'd been holding, Chris quickly walked away and didn't stop until he'd reached the back deck. He grabbed a Coke from one of the coolers and leaned against the rail sipping the cool drink. A gentle breeze blew across his face. He loved fall with all its color changes. A memory of his sister playing in the leaves as a child surfaced and he smiled. Sandra loved having him bury her so she could burst through the pile and have the leaves rain down on her. Chris could still hear her sweet laughter. Just as swiftly, he recalled the yelling and scolding that seemed to always follow and his smile faded. His parents made it their mission to extinguish any bit of joy Chris and Sandra found. He pushed the bitter memories aside.

He heard a loud cheer and glanced over his shoulder to see the two guys they'd beat pumping their fists in the air. Apparently, the king had been dethroned. Chuckling to himself, Chris turned back to the night. A moment later, he heard the sliding glass door open and tensed.

"Hiding from all the ladies, Chris?"

He relaxed. "Leila, I really need you to chill on all this matchmaking."

Leila came and stood next to him. She smiled and shrugged. "I can't help it. I want you to have the same thing Matt and I have. I will admit, though, that Nichelle might not have been the right choice."

Chris snorted. "You think?"

"Alright, but I know another—"

"No more matchmaking." If he didn't stop this madness, she'd figure out a way to introduce him to every single woman in the house. Even now, he could see a couple of them through the glass doors eying him with coy smiles. "Contrary to popular belief, I'm not completely clueless when it comes to women and I'm not hard up for a date." He just chose to deal with them on his own terms.

Leila laughed and raised her hands in mock surrender. "Okay, okay, but you need a wife."

Chris shook his head at her singlemindedness.

She hooked her arm in his. "Since I can't hook you up with a friend, how about a slice of my 7-Up pound cake?"

A smile tilted the corners of his mouth. "Now *that's* an offer I can't refuse."

Inside, Leila cut him a large slice and handed the plate to him. "I admit, being married to Matt has its advantages. I couldn't bake worth a damn before his mother took me under her wing."

"Well, you've mastered this one," he said, placing another bite of the moist cake in his mouth. Growing up, Chris had spent many days at Matt's house to escape the drama at his own. He'd stuffed himself with Mrs. Harris' homemade desserts, and those times had been among his best childhood memories. Someone came and claimed Leila's attention, so Chris stood off to the side enjoying his cake while bobbing his head in time to the rhythm of Cameo's "Word Up."

"You left the table like your drawers were on fire."

He shifted slightly and met Matt's smiling face. "Remind me next time to send my regrets the next time you invite me to one of these things."

White teeth sparkled in Matt's dark face. "Hey, it's not my fault the ladies want to get next to you." He took a sip of his beer. "Any candidates for the title of Mrs. Davis, yet?"

"No." Once again Max's beautiful face flashed in his head.

"Hmm, that's different?"

Chris frowned. "What?"

"The look you just had. Is she anybody I know?"

"I didn't have any look and I have no idea what you're talking about."

"Okay. Go ahead and play dumb. Just remember I've known you your entire life and I can tell when a woman's on your mind. Not that it happens very often, but…" Matt let the sentence hang.

He sighed inwardly. No sense in lying to himself, Max had piqued his interest in a way he couldn't explain. He just hoped he could convince her to talk to him long enough to find out.

CHAPTER 3

"*H*ey, gypsy," Max said when she answered her sister, Teresa's call.

Teresa laughed. "Hey, big sis. Are you busy today?"

"I'm busy every day, and right now I'm on my way to my next client's house. Why?"

"Just hoping we could maybe do a late lunch before I head back to LA for the week. My assignment ends on Saturday. *Hallelujah!*" Teresa Richardson worked as a traveling nurse, and most of her assignments lasted about three months each.

Max signaled and turned into the neighborhood where Sandra lived. With any luck, Mr. Rude wouldn't show up today. "Why didn't you tell me you were going to be in town earlier? I could've moved some things around."

"It was a last minute thing, but I'll be back next Tuesday."

She mentally went over her weekly schedule. "That's a week from now, so let's plan to have lunch on that Friday. I actually have an hour and a half block from one to two-thirty."

"Sounds good. I'll call you when I get back and we can decide where to eat."

"Alright. Are you okay, though?" She couldn't put her finger on it, but something in Teresa's voice gave her pause.

"I'm fine. I thought we'd get through at least one phone call without you asking that question. Guess not," Teresa cracked.

Max smiled as she parked in front of the house. "Hey, I've been looking out for you all your life. It's too late to stop now." At forty-three, Teresa was a decade younger and Max had always been protective of her baby sister. "I'm here, so I have to go. Be safe and we'll talk later."

"You, too. Love you, girl."

"Ditto." Still smiling, she ended the call, then popped the trunk and got out. After filling a large duffle with the toys she'd need, she slung it and a tote on one shoulder and tucked a small exercise ball under the other arm. She hit the foot button to close the trunk on the SUV and sent up a silent thank you to the person who came up with the ingenious idea. Max locked the doors by remote and started up the walk. It didn't take long for the door to open after she rang the bell and she held her breath, hoping not to have a repeat of her last visit.

"Hi, Max." Sandra smiled and held the door open for Max to enter. "Come on back. You're pretty loaded down. Do you want me to carry something for you?"

"Thanks for the offer, but I've got it." Max followed her back and visibly relaxed when she didn't see the woman's brother. Hopefully, he wouldn't drop by until she was long gone.

"Malia just woke up, so I don't know how much she'll do today." As if the little girl knew they were talking about her, Malia looked up from the carrier and gave her a sleepy smile.

"We'll go over my report first and give her a few minutes to wake up." Placing the ball and her bags on the floor, she sat on the sofa and dug a folder out of the tote.

She handed Sandra a copy and kept the other one for herself.

"Do you think Malia will benefit from occupational therapy?" Sandra asked anxiously. "Aside from her pediatrician and social worker, none of the other service providers felt it would be worthwhile."

Max gave her a soft smile. "I do. Let's..." Max trailed off at the sight of Christian entering the room.

"Oh, hey, Chris. You're just in time to hear the result of Max's evaluation," Sandra said, smiling at her brother. To Max she said, "Now I don't have to play twenty questions later because somebody," she gestured toward Christian, "needs to have all the details and then some."

Max was determined to remain professional, no matter what. She took a deep breath. "Mr. Davis, I'm glad you could make it. I know how important your niece's wellbeing is to you." She braced herself for whatever smart-aleck comment he might say.

The corner of his mouth kicked up in a smile. "It's Chris, and you're right."

The intense way he stared at her made her pulse skip. *What the...?* Irritated, she shook herself mentally. Nzinga was right about those damn eyes.

Chris leaned over and kissed his sister's temple, then squatted and placed a kiss on Malia's forehead. "How's my baby girl?" Malia's eyes lit up, and she gave him a bright smile.

Max tried not to let the sweet moment distract her from the fact the man was still a jerk. "I'm sorry I don't have another copy of the report."

He took a seat on the sofa's arm next to his sister. "No problem. I can share with Sandra."

Max nodded and went over each area of her findings, making sure to focus on Malia's strengths, rather than her deficits. Finally, she shared long and short-term goals. When she finished, she asked, "Do either of you have any questions?"

Chris ran a hand down his face. "This seems to be a lot—reaching for toys, keeping her head up and sitting for a few seconds. Right now, she can barely keep her head up for five seconds. What happens if she doesn't reach any of these goals? Will that be the end of therapy? Has this worked with other kids?"

The concern in his voice moved Max. His other faults notwithstanding, it was obvious Chris loved his niece. She read the same apprehensive look on Sandra's face and she sought to reassure them. "These goals are for a year and every child is different. I've had some reach their goals well before the next evaluation period and others who didn't, but made progress on their short-term goals. We can always adjust them, if necessary, and it won't be the end of therapy if she doesn't reach all of them."

"Thank you," Sandra whispered, leaning against Chris. "I like how you said *we*, as if we're a team."

"We are a team. Each week, I'll leave you with a few activities to work on that can be easily incorporated into your day."

"But I'm not a therapist."

Max smiled. Sandra had echoed the concern of another parent. "You're Malia's mother and the only thing you need to do is play with her." She placed the report back into the folder and stuck it into the tote, then got down onto the floor. "Let me show you a few things."

"Okay." Sandra took Malia out of the carrier and lowered herself next to Max.

She took the baby and once Sandra had spread a blanket, laid Malia down on her stomach. Max took the same position in front of the little one and called to her. Malia lifted her head briefly and smiled. The next time, Max used a small toy that made a noise when squeezed to capture her attention and Malia's head stayed up a few seconds longer.

"Oh, my goodness. Look, Chris. She's keeping her head up," Sandra said excitedly.

"I see."

By the end of the hour, Max had shown both Sandra and Chris a few techniques when playing with Malia.

As Max packed up, Sandra said, "I can't believe how well my baby is responding. Thank you so much, Max."

"You're welcome. If you have any questions, just jot them down and we'll go over them when I come next week."

"Alright. Can we keep this time? The afternoon seems to work better for her sleep schedule."

She really wanted to come earlier and, hopefully, avoid seeing Chris, but this wasn't about him. "Sure. This can be your permanent time slot. If you need to cancel, just call the number on my card." Max stood and reached for her duffle.

"I got it." Chris leaped to his feet, then picked up the bag and the ball.

She sighed inwardly, but kept her smile in place. "Thanks. I'll see you next week, Sandra."

"After you," he said and followed her out to the car.

Max said nothing as she opened the trunk, took the ball and bag and deposited them inside. "You really didn't have to carry this out. I do it every day."

"I know, but I wanted to talk to you."

She lifted a brow and folded her arms. "About?"

"I owe you an apology for my less than stellar behavior last week."

"Less than stellar, huh? That's what you're calling it? Well, you're going to need to climb several notches to reach *less than stellar*."

"Ouch," Chris said with a smile. "You don't pull any punches."

"Nope."

"Seeing as how I need to climb a steep hill, would you allow me to apologize over dinner? That is if you're not seeing anyone."

"You're asking me out?" Max asked with surprise. She didn't know what she expected him to say, but asking her out never crossed her mind. "And no, I'm not seeing anyone. And since you're asking, I assume you're single."

"Yes to both your questions, and I promise to be on my very best behavior."

"I don't date my clients."

Chris took a step closer to Max. "If I'm not mistaken, you work with children. I can assure you that my kid days are long gone. And the baby you're referring to is not mine, so I don't see any conflict of interest."

The timbre of his deep voice and those hazel eyes framed by long lashes women would sell their souls for had her heart beating a mile a minute. She was so tempted, and technically, he was correct. But still, he looked a little too young for her. "How old are you?" She searched his clean-shaven face for any age lines and his close-cropped hair for signs of gray strands, but found none.

Chuckling, he said, "Definitely old enough for you, but to answer your question, I'll be hitting the big five-o in a few months. I would ask you the same, but I've put my foot in my mouth enough."

"Ah, yeah, you don't want to go there." Knowing that there was only a three-year difference in their ages made her feel better. Normally, she would have no qualms about accepting a date offer, especially with a man as fine as Christian. However, lately, she just didn't want to have to deal with the drama she had encountered with romantic relationships. *I must be getting old.*

"So, will you have dinner with me?"

Max couldn't remember the last time she'd gone out on with a man. She studied him for a moment, then decided to bite the bullet. One dinner couldn't hurt. "Okay." She dug her wallet out of her tote.

"Nice wallet. I see you're a fan of Wakanda."

She smiled. "Who isn't? Wakanda forever." She had purchased the Black Panther wallet and purse as soon as she'd seen it. His low rumble vibrated through her, shocking her in the process and she forgot what she was saying for a moment. "This one is getting a little worn, but I haven't been able to find another one." She handed him a business card. "You can call my cell number."

"I'll call you to see what your schedule is like and we'll go from there."

Max closed the trunk. "That apology and dinner better be good. And before we go any further, I'm not into playing games."

A sexy grin curved Chris' mouth. "That's one thing I can absolutely guarantee, Ms. Richardson. And I've never played head games, so you don't have to worry."

Oh, my! She needed to get away from this man, and quick. He made her feel things she'd long forgotten. "One more thing."

"What's that?"

"Do you plan to show up every week?"

He threw his head back and laughed, then shrugged. "Since this is my house...probably."

His house? Great. If things didn't work out, she didn't want to run the risk of seeing him all the time. "I have to go." She unlocked the car and before she could reach the driver side, he was there and had her door open.

Still smiling, he said, "Have a nice afternoon, Max."

"You, too." He closed the door and stood there until she pulled off.

By the time she got home, Max was still thinking about Chris. With his towering height and good looks, she'd be lying if she said she wasn't attracted to him. And she knew it was mutual. The intensity of his stare gave him away. Pushing the thoughts away, she dumped all the toys she'd used into the kitchen sink and filled it with warm, soapy water. She made a practice of washing her toys every evening to remove any lingering germs the antibacterial wipes left behind.

While the toys soaked, she entered her notes for each client into the online system. Afterward, she rinsed the toys and placed them on a towel to dry. Afterward, she placed two salmon filets into a Ziploc bag with a mesquite and teriyaki marinade, then set it in the refrigerator to chill for a few minutes.

Max had just gotten comfortable with a mystery novel when her doorbell rang. Sighing, she made her way to the front. Lately, the neighborhood had seen an increase in solicitors and she made a mental note to pick up one of those "no solicitors" signs. She opened the door and let out a soft gasp. "Dion!"

"Hey, Mom. Can I come in?"

"Of course, baby." She quickly unlocked the screen and held it open. She hadn't seen him since the summer and she missed him. At an even six feet, he eclipsed her height by four inches. She desperately wanted to hug him, but didn't for fear that he would side-step it as he'd done since buying into his father's lies. Dion reached out to hug Max, shocking her in the process. He held onto her as if she were his lifeline and she felt the tears stinging her eyes. "Are you okay?" she asked, leaning back and searching his face.

Dion shook his head. "I…"

She took his hand and led him to the family room. "Have a seat and tell me what's going on." Despite things being strained between them, he was her baby, her only child, and she would walk through the fire for him.

He sat on the sofa next to her, bowed his head and rested his clasped hands on his thighs. "I don't even know where to begin. Mom, I'm *so sorry* for how I've treated you," he whispered brokenly. "I was wrong, and I don't even know how you'll ever be able to forgive what I've done."

The tears Max had held back spilled over before she could stop them. She had waited so long to be reconciled with her son. "Honey, I love you, and I always will."

"I know, and I feel worse. I should've known you would never do the things Dad accused you of doing. In my heart, I knew. I *knew*, but I still listened to his lies."

Max went still. "What are you talking about?"

Dion lifted his eyes. "You didn't cheat. Dad did."

She sat stunned, not knowing what to say. So she said nothing, and waited for him to continue.

"He got married on Saturday. All this time, he made it seem like he and Gayle hooked up after the two of you broke up. But it was all a lie. During the ceremony, the minister said he'd been praying for their marriage to happen for the last seven years," he said bitterly. "I'm not stupid and I can do the math. You and Dad have only been divorced six years, which means he was the one who screwed up our family, not you."

"Dion."

"No, Mom. Just tell me the truth. *Please.*"

Max released a deep sigh. "Yes, he was the one who cheated."

Dion buried his head in his hands. "Why didn't you tell

me before? Why didn't you say something when he kept lying? I messed up," he muttered over and over.

The misery reflected in Dion's face broke her heart. She scooted closer to him and placed a comforting arm around his shoulders. "Dion, what happened was between your father and me. It was bad enough with him trying to make you choose sides. The last thing I was going to do is make it worse by doing the same." She'd tried to get her ex to keep the drama between them and to not involve their son, but he'd been so hell-bent on making her look like the bad guy that he wouldn't listen. Max had told Rolando karma was going to come back to bite him on the ass and her prediction had been right. "There's nothing to forgive, baby. I will always, *always* be here for you, no matter what."

"Even though I acted like a butthead according to Monique." He shook his head. "She tried to tell me to stay out of grown folks business and that things were probably not as cut and dried as I believed. I should have listened."

At three years older, her goddaughter had a good head on her shoulders. Monique and Dion had grown up together and she treated Dion like a younger brother. "You're here now and that's all that matters."

"Thanks, Mom."

"For what?"

"For making this so easy. It took me a week to get up the guts to come and talk to you. After how I acted, I wasn't sure you'd want to see me." Dion shook his head again and blew out a long breath. "I love you, Mom, and I promise I'll make it up to you."

She gave him a soft smile. To say she had been hurt by his behavior would be an understatement, but Max couldn't and wouldn't hold it against him. Dion had only been listening to the man he'd looked up to and should have been trustworthy.

"Don't worry about trying to make anything up. Just promise me you'll talk to me if you have concerns about anything."

"I promise."

"Does your father know?"

"Yes. I confronted him at the reception, and he still tried to lie, so I left. He's been calling, but I don't want to hear anything he has to say."

Max heard the anger in his voice, and as much as she wanted to co-sign, he didn't need that. "I understand how upset you are, Dion, but you're going to have to let it go. Otherwise, it will eat you alive, and I don't want that for you."

Dion eyed her. "Yeah, well, it's going to take a while for me to get there. Make that a long while. I'm just glad I moved out last month. Right now I don't want to talk to him or see him."

"You moved? Where?"

He ducked his head sheepishly. "Sorry, Mom. I found a one-bedroom apartment in Natomas. Maybe you can come to dinner sometime."

She lifted an eyebrow. "Are you planning to cook and will it be edible?" Her son's claim to culinary fame consisted of ramen noodles, canned chili, frozen fish sticks and peanut butter and jelly sandwiches. His laughter exploded and the sound warmed her heart. Max had been afraid she wouldn't ever hear it again.

"Okay, okay, I'll give you that one. You'll be happy to know that I've learned to cook, and I have to say I do a pretty good job," he said with a smile.

Max returned his smile and bumped his shoulder. "Then I'll be waiting for my invitation." She opened her mouth to say something else and her cell rang. Reaching over to the small end table, she picked it up, but didn't recognize the number. Because it could be one of her parents canceling, she decided to answer. "Hello."

"Hey, Max. It's Chris."

"Chris. Hey." His voice sounded even deeper over the phone. And sexy.

"I'm calling to see whether you'll be available this weekend for dinner. Friday or Saturday is fine with me."

She hadn't expected him to call less than two hours after leaving, but it earned him a few brownie points. "Friday works better for me."

"Is seven too late? I know you have to work and I wanted to give you time to get home and relax."

Another point earned. "Seven sounds good. Casual or dressy?"

"Definitely dressy. It's our first date, and I'm trying to get out of that ditch."

Max laughed. "Well, you're doing okay so far. We'll see how the rest goes."

Chris chuckled. I'll go with that. You have my number now. Please text me your address. I'm looking forward to spending the evening with you."

"Same," she said softly. Why was her heart beating so fast? "I'll see you Friday." She disconnected and turned to see Dion staring at her with a curious smile. "What?"

"You have a boyfriend?"

"If I did, would it be a problem?"

Dion shook his head. "Not at all. You deserve to be happy."

"We just met, so he's not a boyfriend, as you put it."

"Does he have potential?"

Sexy voice, killer smile, fine as wine… Yeah, potential. "I'll let you know." She stood and started toward the kitchen. "I'm making salmon if you want to stay for dinner," she called over her shoulder.

He hopped up and was on her heels. "Mom, I haven't eaten your cooking for *six* long years. I definitely want to stay. I'll even help. What are we having with it?"

Laughing, Max shrugged. "Some kind of potatoes and whatever vegetable is in the refrigerator."

"Potatoes and vegetables? That I can do." He slung an arm around her shoulder and kissed her cheek. "I missed you."

"I missed you, too, baby boy." She patted his cheek. Max had her son back and a date with a sexy man. Life was pretty good right now.

CHAPTER 4

*F*riday afternoon, Christian headed out of the station to his car.

"Hey, Davis. Wait up."

He turned and saw Nathan McGee striding toward him. "What's up?" he asked as the man approached.

Nathan fell into step with Chris. "You're in a hurry to leave today."

He chuckled. "I'm always in a hurry to leave work." Although, he would be the first to admit today he'd finished his debriefing and paperwork, changed out of his uniform and was out the door quicker than usual because of his date with Max later. He tried to recall the last time he'd been so anxious to spend time with a woman and couldn't.

"I wanted to ask if you planned to apply for the sergeant position."

"I haven't decided." The promotion would definitely boost his pension, but on the flip side, he'd have to start at the bottom again and most likely end up on a graveyard shift again. After more than twenty years, his seniority afforded him the coveted day shift and no weekends, and Chris wasn't sure he wanted to give that up, especially at his age. And now he had to factor Max into the equation, as well. He had no idea how things would turn out, but trying to begin a relationship while balancing opposite work schedules could potentially end things before they could start. And he definitely didn't want that to happen, especially now that he'd found a woman he wanted to get to know. "What about you?"

"Maybe. The pay increase sure would be nice," Nathan said with a grin.

Chris stopped at his truck. "No doubt."

"You want to go grab a couple of beers tonight? A buddy of mine turned me on to this place where lots of beautiful women hang out. *Single* women."

A few years ago, he might have taken Nate up on his invitation. However, the older he got, the less picking up women in a bar or frequenting dance clubs appealed to him. "Nah, I'm good."

"Man, you aren't getting any younger. You never know. You might find a wife."

Chris snorted as he unlocked the door by remote. "You've been going for the past few months and it hasn't helped you, so I'll pass." Besides, marriage wasn't on his radar. He'd been there, done it, crashed and burned. Even if he thought about making another trip down the aisle, it would have to be with someone like Max. Her intelligence, compassion and beauty had totally captivated him. And every time he saw her voluptuous body in those fitted knit pants, made him want to caress each curve.

"Yeah, well, that just means I haven't met her yet," Nate said with a laugh. "No pain, no gain, as they say."

He slid in behind the wheel. "Good luck and let me know if you find her. Later."

"I'll do that. You can be my best man." Nathan threw up a wave and continued to his car.

Chris shook his head, started the engine and pulled out onto the road. He had to pick up his suit from the cleaners and stop at a florist for flowers, something he'd heard some of the younger officers say had gone out of style. Granted, he didn't make a practice of buying flowers for every woman he'd taken out. However, there was something different and special about Max, and being old school, he wanted to let her know. It was also his way of apologizing. As he drove, he admitted to himself that he wanted to make a good impression tonight. His first meeting with Max had been so far out of character for him and, for reasons he didn't understand at the moment, he wanted her to get to know the real him.

After leaving the dry cleaners, Chris walked into the florist shop and stared at the many different floral arrangements. He slowly made his way around the small space and finally settled on a small bouquet of pink roses.

"Hey, big bro," Sandra said when Chris walked in the house.

Chris kissed her cheek. "Hey. Where's Malia?" He placed the flowers in the refrigerator.

"She's taking a nap. A suit and flowers? You must have a hot date tonight." She folded her arms and leaned against the counter with a smile on her face.

"Something like that." He hadn't told her about his dinner with Max because despite her own marriage's demise, his sister was a diehard romantic and she would figure out a way to play matchmaker.

She followed him to his bedroom. "That's all you're going to say?"

He hung the suit up, then sat to remove his shoes. "What exactly is it you want me to say, Sandy?"

"The usual. What's her name, where did you meet her, is

she pretty, what does she look like, and where are you going?"

Chuckling, Chris shook his head. "I see nothing has changed from when you were a nosy kid." Growing up, whenever he got ready to go out, she would be on his heels, asking those same questions and more, trying to pick out his clothes, and giving him pointers on where he should take a girl for dinner.

Sandra dropped down on the bed beside him and play-fully bumped his shoulder. "Come on, Chris. Who is she and why are you being so secretive?" She narrowed her gaze. "This woman isn't one of those high-maintenance chicks like Taryn, is she?" She wrinkled her nose as if she'd smelled something bad.

"No," he answered emphatically. He'd gone out with Taryn once. The woman had complained about his choice of restaurant, the food, the other patrons, the service, then had the nerve to ask him if he could pay her car note because she was a little short on money for the month. Her excuse had been that she'd had to purchase a new outfit so she could look good for him. Chris had been so outdone, he cut the night short, took her home and walked away without a back-ward glance. That had been more than a year ago and he hadn't taken a woman out since then, preferring to skip the drama that came along with dating.

"Well? I can't believe you're still not saying."

He pushed to his feet. "Let me get this first one out of the way and if there's a potential for more, we'll talk."

"Fine, but I expect some details *tomorrow*, regardless of how the night ends."

The sound of Malia's cry interrupted their conversation. "I'll get her." Chris rushed out of the room before Sandra could say anything. He smiled down at his niece lying in her crib and lifted her into his arms. "Hey, baby girl. What's all the fussing about?" He placed a soft kiss on her forehead. "You're okay," he crooned while gently rocking her. The cries turned into a whimper, then stopped altogether within seconds. Chris carried her back down the hallway, still talking to her while she gazed up at him contentedly.

"I don't know how you always do that," Sandra grumbled. "It takes me a good three or four minutes to calm her down. Yet, you walk in the room and she immediately stops crying. It's a shame you never had any children of your own. You'd make a great dad."

He'd wanted children early in his life, but had put the desire away once he realized it would never happen. Now he was just satisfied with being an uncle. "Your mama's jealous," he said to Malia. As if she'd understood his words, Malia smiled and cooed. He winked at Sandra. "See, she knows Uncle Chris is the best."

She rolled her eyes. "Give me my baby and go get ready for your *secret* date."

Laughing, he handed her the baby. "Don't hate." She swatted at him, but he sidestepped the blow.

"You see how your uncle treats me?" she asked Malia. "Oh, I almost forgot to tell you today she kept her head up for almost fifteen seconds while we were playing on the floor. All the things Max suggested are helping already and I'm so excited. I can't wait to tell her when she comes next week."

He smiled. "That's great news. I'm sure she'll be glad to hear it." Chris could very well pass along the information to Max when he picked her up, but tonight wasn't about business. Just pleasure. He also didn't want to deprive his sister of sharing the good news. It was the first time since Malia's birth that he'd seen hope in his sister's eyes and he had Max to thank.

Two hours later, Chris parked in front of Max's one-story

house and went to ring the doorbell. Anything he'd planned to say went right out the window when she opened the door wearing a knee-length navy dress that dipped just low enough in the front to give a hint of cleavage and skimmed every one of her delectable curves. She'd twisted her natural curls into an elegant updo and had added a touch of makeup to her already beautiful face. The deep burgundy shade of lipstick was so enticing, it took all his control not to kiss her and see if her lips were as soft as they looked.

Max laughed softly. "Are you going to stand there all night staring, or do you want to come in?"

A smile curved his lips. "I think I'd like to do both. You are absolutely stunning, Max."

Her gaze made a slow path down his body and back up again. "You clean up pretty nicely yourself, Chris. Come on in. I just need to grab my purse and coat."

He stepped inside and handed her the flowers. "These are for you."

"Thank you. They're beautiful. I think you just climbed one step up from your ditch."

"That's good to know," he said with a chuckle. "Hopefully, I'll be able to see the top of the hole by the end of the night."

"Well, this is a good start. Have a seat. I'm going to put these pretty babies in a vase, and I'll be right back."

Chris watched the sway of her hips and her shapely legs until she was out of sight, then lowered himself onto the sofa. *What a woman!* A blaze lit inside him. He wiped at the perspiration dotting his brow and had the sudden urge to loosen his tie. Each time he saw Max, his attraction to her grew. Thankfully, it wasn't one-sided. He knew she felt the chemistry between them as strongly as he did. Chris stood as Max entered the room, eased the coat from her, and helped her put it on.

Max smiled up at him. "Thanks. Ready?"

"Very." He was more than ready for whatever the evening brought.

Max sat beside Chris in the cozy confines of his Audi sedan and tried to settle the butterflies in her stomach. Her friends, especially Nzinga, would probably hurt themselves laughing if they knew how nervous Max felt at the moment. Of the quartet, she tended to be the most outspoken and daring when it came to men. Yet, somehow, something about the man behind the wheel had her uncharacteristically behaving like a shy teen. When she'd told him he cleaned up nicely, it had been an understatement. With her five-eight height, she typically stood eye level with the men she'd gone out with when she dressed up. Not so this time. Even in her three-inch heels, he still towered over her by almost half a foot, and she liked it. She'd thought him impressive in his uniform and in a pair of jeans, but the charcoal gray suit caressing his tall, slender frame left no doubt in her mind that it had been tailored expressly for him, making him look good enough to eat. And she could admit she wouldn't mind sampling his very sexy menu. Deciding she needed to get a grip, Max asked, "Where are we going?"

"I made reservations at Morton's downtown." Chris slanted her a quick glance. "Is that okay?"

"Better than okay." Flowers, an expensive steakhouse... the man was racking up brownie points faster than she could count them. She smiled. *I'm down with that.* Max made herself comfortable in the soft leather seat and focused her attention on the passing scenery while listening to the soft jazz coming through the speakers.

After several minutes of companionable silence, he asked, "Did you have a long day?"

She shifted her gaze his way. "Not really. I had a couple of cancellations which shortened my day to two o'clock. But I'm meeting with my friend, who owns the clinic to talk about decreasing my hours. This body is getting a little old for a forty-hour workweek. All that getting down and up from the floor starts to take its toll after a while." It would also give her the opportunity to get in a little more "me time" and not have to cram it all in on Saturdays.

"You're not that old."

"I'm old enough and we'll just leave it at that." They shared a brief smile before he turned his attention back to the road.

"Since I'm still making my way out of that ditch, my lips are sealed," Chris said with a laugh. "How long have you been a therapist?"

"Almost twenty-eight years."

"All of it with children?"

"In one setting or another, yes. I've worked in the clinic, schools and the home. My favorite, by far, is the birth to three population, which is why I'm seeing your niece. I get to watch them grow and progress over the course of two or more years and it's so cool to see their eyes light up when they learn a new skill for the first time."

"From what I've seen these past couple of weeks, you're amazing at what you do."

"Thanks. That's high praise coming from you." Max couldn't help but recall their first meeting. Looking back, she could understand his frustrations, but she still didn't have to like that he'd taken them out on her. However, he was doing a good job making up for his previous behavior. The conversation tapered off as he pulled into an outdoor lot in downtown Sacramento.

"I prepaid parking here since it's the closest to the restaurant. Will you be okay walking a short distance? If not, I can drop you off in front and come back and park."

She waved him off. "I appreciate the offer, but I'll be fine." Morton's was directly across the street. She watched as he came around to help her out of the car. Why hadn't she noticed his sexy walk before? Chris extended his hand and gently pulled her to her feet, then closed and locked the door. They'd gone several steps before she realized he hadn't let go of her hand. It had been such a long time since she'd held hands with a man, she had almost forgotten how it felt. His warm grip was strong and sure, just like the man striding next to her. Once they entered the restaurant, it only took a few minutes for them to be seated. Chris waited until she slid in the booth, then sat opposite her. The hostess handed them menus, then departed. Max picked up her menu. A moment later, the server arrived to take their drink order. Both opted for a Cabernet. "I've only been here once years ago and I don't remember what I had," she said after the young woman departed. "What's good?"

"Your guess is good as mine," Chris said, staring intently at her over his menu. "You're the first woman I've brought here."

Her pulse skipped. She took a sip of her water to cover her rising attraction. "So what, you usually take your dates to McDonald's or something?"

His low rumble of laughter floated across the table. "Not at all. But I wanted tonight to be special, particularly since I have a two-fold mission."

Max angled her head. "What kind of mission?"

Chris lowered his menu and the corner of his mouth kicked up in smile. "My first mission is the apology. The second," he leaned forward and clasped his hands on the table, "is to get to know you better."

He really needed to stop looking at her with those eyes.

She could feel herself being drawn in to his sensual web every time he glanced her way. "Apology accepted."

His smile widened. "Thank you. And just to be clear, it's going to take more than one dinner for us to get to know each other."

"We haven't even made it through this one yet. You might change your mind by the end of the night," she added with a laugh.

"I don't think so. The only thing I'm going to want at the end of the night is a promise of more time with you." Chris tossed her bold wink and picked up his menu again.

Well, alrighty then. A man who knew what he wanted. Max could only smile as she perused the food selections. "I really want the ribeye, but the smallest cut is still too big."

"If you're okay with us sharing, we can order the twenty-two ounce bone-in."

She gave him a dazzling smile. "Perfect." The server returned with their drinks and took their food order. Along with their steak, they decided to share sides of grilled asparagus, sour cream mashed potatoes and sautéed mushrooms.

He handed the server the menu. "Can you please bring us an extra plate, as well?"

The woman nodded and walked away.

"Since we played twenty questions with me, it's your turn," Max said. "Why did you choose your career?"

Chris took a sip of his wine. "It wasn't my first choice. I majored in criminal justice with the intention of going to law school. But after my father was killed while driving drunk, I switched gears, and after graduating, went to the CHP academy. I wanted to keep people like him off the streets."

She could hear the pain and anger in his voice and her heart went out to him. His shuttered gaze also made her think there was more to the story, but she didn't know him well enough to ask. "I'm sorry."

"It's okay."

"Do you like what you do? I imagine it can be difficult."

A wry grin touched his lips. "Some days are worse than others. I see people on their worsr day, especially when it involves an accident and there's a fatality. It takes its toll, and I've had to learn how to compartmentalize and not bring it home."

Max completely understood. Without thinking, she reached over and covered his hand. "Thank you for what you do to try to keep our streets safer." With his gaze locked on hers, he placed a lingering kiss on the back of her hand. Heat shot up her arm. She eased her hand out of his and took a hasty gulp of her wine. *What in the world is going on?* Thankfully, their food arrived and they could table the emotional conversation.

"How much of the steak do you want?"

She glanced over at the huge steak and used her knife to indicate. He cut off her portion and placed in on the extra plate. He waited for her to add the side dishes before filling his own. For the first few minutes, they ate in silence.

"How is it?" Chris asked.

"So good. And this steak…mmm. I must not be buying the right kind of steaks because mine are never this tender."

He smiled. "That's because you probably buy your meat from the grocery store. These are prime grade steaks. Most stores tend to carry choice cuts, which aren't bad, but these," he pointed to his steak, "are much better." He angled his head thoughtfully. "How about I buy a couple and throw them on the grill for us sometime soon?"

Max leaned back in her seat. "You can cook?"

"Of course I can cook," Chris said, giving her a look of disbelief. "I like to eat. I grill, sauté, fry, bake…all of it. Besides, eating out every day can get really expensive."

"I happen to be free next Friday."

"So am I. Same time?"

She nodded. "Same bat channel."

Grinning, he said, "You've got Marvel and DC comics down to a science, I see."

Max shrugged. "What can I say? I love a good superhero."

Chris angled his head thoughtfully. "Is that all you love?"

"I guess you'll have to find out," she said, taking a sip of her wine.

"I guess I will. So do we have a date for next Friday?"

She gave him a bright smile. "We do. Although, I'm going to have to watch what I eat all week, so I can be ready."

"I try to watch what I eat most times, as well. However, I'm not opposed to indulging in a sweet, delectable dessert every now and again," he added, his voice deepening and his eyes sparkling with desire.

"Is that right? Hmm…sounds tempting."

"Let me know when you're ready to…*indulge*."

Somehow the conversation had shifted from food to something completely different and she felt the heat rising between them. Max resisted the urge to fan herself. She had never played these kind of word games with her ex, or any other man for that matter. But she found the sensual banter stimulating. "I'll be ready whenever you are." She went back to her food, finding her dining partner more fascinating by the moment. Never would she have believed that beneath the bad-mannered, glaring man she'd met that first day was a man who could turn her on just with a look. As if on cue, the server returned as they finished the meal. She left a dessert menu and cleared away the empty dishes.

"So, are you up for a little dessert?" Chris asked.

"Are we sharing?" The words left her mouth before she could stop them. That heart-stopping smile appeared on his face again.

"Absolutely. I'll let you choose our dessert."

Why is it so warm in here? Max picked up her water and nearly drained the glass, then stared at the selection. "I think I'd like the legendary hot chocolate cake with ice cream."

"Chocolate. My favorite." Chris placed the order and waited for the server to leave before saying, "Do you have a sweet tooth?"

"Sometimes, but chocolate is my weakness."

"I'm starting to think it's mine, too," he murmured.

Once the dessert arrived, she decided it might not have been a good idea for them to share. With his searing gaze focused on her as they ate, each bite of the delicious cake had her melting just like its chocolate center. After finishing, they sat there laughing and talking for another hour.

When they made it back to her place, she debated whether to invite him in. She'd enjoyed herself and wasn't quite ready for the evening to end. "Would you like to come in?"

"For a few minutes." Chris waited for her to unlock the door, followed her in and closed it behind him.

"Can I get you anything?" Max asked, walking toward the sofa and dropping her purse onto a chair.

"Actually, yes." He slid an arm around her waist and drew her into his embrace. "I might be a little rusty since it's been a while, but I'd really like to kiss you. Would that be okay?"

"Yes," she whispered. Before she got the word out good, he swooped down and captured her lips in a deep, passionate kiss that stole her breath and weakened her knees. His tongue tangled around hers making sweeping, swirling motions in her mouth. She moaned. Her hands roamed over the solid wall of his chest and wound around his neck. This time, she heard him groan and she shuddered. At length, he lifted his head. Max rested her head against his shoulder and tried to get her breathing under control. She felt the rapid pace of his heartbeat matching hers as Chris held her protectively against his hard body, his hands slowly moving up and down her back.

"I should probably leave," he said after some time, although he didn't attempt to let her go. Finally, he eased back, but kept her close. "I really enjoyed dinner with you, Max, and I'm looking forward to seeing you again."

Looking up at him, she smiled. "So did I, and same here."

Chris returned her smile and brushed a kiss over her lips. "We can go out if you prefer, or I can cook like I mentioned earlier."

"I think I might want to sample that steak you mentioned."

He pulled her closer. "Deal. Friday at seven it is." He took her hand and walked back to the front.

"Thanks for dinner. You more than made your way out of that ditch."

Chuckling, he said, "That's good to know. Hopefully, I can keep myself out of it." He opened the door and stepped out onto the porch.

"Oh, and I can't wait until you get up to full speed with your kisses if that's what you call *rusty*."

"Well, they say practice makes perfect, so…"

The kiss that followed was filled with a sweetness that sent a myriad of sensations flowing through Max.

"How's that?"

"Better."

He kissed her one last time. "Goodnight, Max."

"Night, Chris." She watched him lope down the three steps and walkway to his car. He threw up a wave. She returned it, then closed the door and let out a soft sigh.

She retrieved her purse and nearly floated down the hallway to her bedroom. Sitting on the side of the bed, she took off her shoes, then dug her phone out of her purse to send a text to her friends: *Y'all will be happy to know that I decided to go out with Mr. Rude. I changed my mind...I like him!* In less than three minutes, the phone rang. Max smiled when she saw Val's name on the display.

"How did I know you'd be the first to respond?" she asked when she connected.

Val's laughter came through the line. "Because Nzinga is probably snuggled up with Byron and Donna is most likely in bed already, even though it's barely eleven o'clock. But that's beside the point. I want details and don't leave anything out."

Max made herself comfortable on the bed and just like she'd done when they were teenagers, spent the next several minutes giving her friend a play by play of the evening, starting with how he'd asked her out, their banter over dinner, and ending with the heated kisses.

"Girl, you've got me over here fanning," Val said. "I've got to give him props. Morton's on the first date is setting the bar pretty high. I like a man who doesn't mind pulling out all the stops."

"Yeah, I kind of like him, too."

"And those kisses?"

"He said he was rusty because he hadn't done it in a while, but *mercy*, if that's how he kisses when he's out of practice, I don't know if I can handle him when he's up to speed."

Val screamed with laughter. "But I know you're going to try."

"You'd better believe it." Even now, she could still feel the softness of his lips on hers. Yeah, she'd handle it. And enjoy every one of those *practice* sessions. Practice made perfect, indeed.

CHAPTER 5

"Come on, Max. Think about it. If you become co-owner, you can cut your caseload down by half."

"And triple my paperwork. You know how much I hate doing reports. What makes you think I'm going to willingly add more to my load?" Max stared across her desk and shook her head at the singlemindedness of her friend and boss, Caroline Townsend. The two had worked together for another pediatric therapy company and became good friends. Both had gotten fed up with the mismanagement of money, resulting in bounced checks and random lapses in medical insurance when the owners didn't pay their share of the premiums on time. When Caroline approached Max with the idea of opening her own clinic ten years ago, Max hadn't hesitated to follow her. It turned out to be the best career decision she'd ever made. No drama, no stress, and no bounced checks. Over the past year, her friend had been trying to convince Max to become a partner, but that would mean more time in an office and less time doing what she loved—playing with her babies.

Caroline rolled her eyes. "I thought you were my friend."

She laughed. "I am your friend and I love working with you, but I don't want to increase my hours. In fact, I wanted to talk to you about reducing them."

Her eyes widened. "You're not talking about retiring soon, are you?"

"No."

"Thank goodness," Caroline said, blowing out a long breath.

"You just hired a new OT, Carol, and she needs to build her caseload, so it's perfect timing. I'm thinking twenty-eight to thirty hours a week. I have four kids aging out at the end of the month and that'll free at least two of my afternoons. I'd like to work six hours a day Monday through Thursday and four on Friday."

"That's doable," she grumbled. "I still say you should think about my offer."

"If you had asked me ten years ago, I might have said yes."

"Damn. I don't know why I didn't think about that then." Caroline sighed dramatically.

Shaking her head and smiling, Max said, "I think you missed your calling, girlfriend. You should be on a stage somewhere, instead of an office." Her phone buzzed. She picked it up off her desk and saw a text from Chris. *Are you going to be home later? I'd like to stop by.* It had been five days since their night out and although they had talked twice, she did want to see him and sent back a quick reply: *Yes. I should be home around four-thirty.*

"Why are you smiling like that? Did you meet somebody and didn't tell me? You know Mike wanted to introduce you to one of the guys at his office."

Caroline's attorney husband had been trying to hook Max up with one colleague or another over the years and constantly invited her to weekend get-togethers, but she hadn't found one of them to be to her liking. "Yes."

She bounced in her chair. "What does he look like and how long have you two been dating?"

"We went out for the first time last Friday."

"It is Wednesday, Max. I've seen you three times since then and you haven't said one word. I can't believe you didn't bring him over to the house on Saturday. I want to meet the man who has you smiling for a change." Caroline knew all about the hell Max had gone through with her ex and her resistance to begin dating again.

"You've met him already." Caroline froze and Max smiled. "Sandra Jones' brother."

Her hand went to her mouth. "Let me get this straight. You went out with the man who had you ranting in here three weeks ago? I thought he was a rude jerk. I mean, I understand, though. He came to the IFSP meeting and the brother is fine, fine, *fine*. And I hope you're not going to use the excuse that you can't go out with him because he's a client because, technically, Sandra is Malia's parent, not him. His name isn't listed on one thing indicating he's a guardian."

The Individualized Family Service Plan was a written plan developed by a team usually consisting of a social worker, therapists and parents that documented the services and goals that would best benefit the infant or toddler. Max had had another client scheduled at the time and missed the meeting. In hindsight, she was glad because she definitely might have turned him down cold. She recalled the sound of his voice when she tried to pull the I-can't-date-my-client card. *I can assure you that my kid days are long gone. And the baby you're referring to is not mine, so I don't see any conflict of interest.* "I didn't, and we're going out again." Or staying in. She didn't know how she felt about going over to his house with his sister living there—a client—and wondered if he'd be opposed to grilling at her place instead. She'd ask when he came over later.

The receptionist stuck her head in Max's office. "Carol, your three o'clock is here."

Caroline hopped up and headed for the door. "Thanks. I'll be there in a second." To Max she said, "Keep me posted and let me know if I need to buy a new dress for the wedding."

Max whipped her head around. "Hold up, crazy woman. Nobody's talking marriage. We're going on a *date*. That. Is. All."

"So you say," she said in singsong as she walked out, her laughter trailing.

Marriage wasn't on her radar and she didn't know if it would ever be, but she planned to enjoy her time with Chris for the time being. She finished entering her notes on the computer, shut everything down and packed up to leave. Her plans to go walking that afternoon would most likely change now that Chris would be visiting. The late October temperatures had climbed into the seventies and she wanted to take advantage of them before it turned cold again. Max typically walked at least three days a week, along with a couple days of weight training to keep her body somewhat in shape. However, the older she got, the more difficult it became, and the workouts she'd done ten or fifteen years ago didn't yield the same results now. As she passed the treatment room where Caroline sat working with her client, Max waved and mouthed, "See you later."

Because the clinic was located a few miles from her house, it took her less than fifteen minutes to get home. *Maybe I should consider the partnership, as it would definitely shorten my commute time and save on gas*, she mused. Max checked the time. She still had a good half hour before Chris got there and toyed with going on a short power walk. Just as quickly, she dismissed the idea because she wouldn't have time to shower.

Max finished drying the last toy as the doorbell rang.

Taking a deep, calming breath, she made her way to the front and opened the door. She had no idea why this one man made her heart race every single time she saw him. Today he wore a pair of well-worn jeans, a black tee that showed off his muscular biceps and running shoes. "Hi." She held the screen open and moved aside for him to enter. Without her heels, her head came to his chest.

"Hey, beautiful." Chris smiled, leaned down and placed a soft kiss on her lips.

"I think I'm enjoying all this practicing," she said, leading him to the family room at the back of the house. She sat on the sofa and patted the space next to her. "Have a seat. Would you like something to drink?"

"No, thanks. I'm good." He lowered himself next to her and glanced around. "You have small children?"

Max laughed. She had lined the toys on a towel to let them finish air drying. "No way. Those are my work toys. My son is twenty-three. Do you have any children?" They hadn't gotten around to this conversation the other night.

"Nope. Just my niece." He pointed to a framed photo on the fireplace. "Is that your son?"

"Yes. That's from his college graduation last May." It had been the only picture she'd captured that day. When Dion stood posing for his father, Max had whipped out her phone and snapped a few shots in rapid succession. She'd chosen that one because his wide and open smile reminded her of better days.

"He favors you a lot."

"Thank goodness."

Chris chuckled. "I take it there's no love lost between you and your ex."

"You take it right." Changing the subject, she asked, "How did your day go?"

He smiled knowingly. "Not too bad. I did have a woman

start crying hysterically when I stopped her for speeding. Of course, it stopped and turned into anger when she realized her tears wouldn't get her out of a ticket."

Max's mouth fell open. "Are you serious?"

"You'd be surprised how many women try that stunt. I've even had a few men start crying because they didn't want the ticket on their driving record."

She shook her head. "That is too funny. Hmm…maybe I should try that the next time I get stopped." The serious look on his face made her laugh. She patted his thigh. "Oh relax. I'm just kidding."

His face broke out into a smile. "You are something else."

"Who me?" She placed a hand over her chest for emphasis. "Nah, I'm just me."

"And I like just you, Ms. Maxine Richardson."

Immediately, the mood shifted and the chemistry between them rose. For a long moment, he stared at her, seemingly trying to determine something, then he leaned closer until their lips were a breath apart. She realized he was waiting for her to make the decision. Why hadn't she met him long ago? So far, he hadn't acted as if he was entitled to her kisses and her body like the other men she'd encountered after her divorce. Instead, he made sure she was comfortable with the pace of the relationship even though she could tell he wanted her. The intensity of his gaze told her all she needed to know. She wanted the kiss as much as he did and touched her lips to his. He cradled her face between his big hands and slowly, but thoroughly, devoured her mouth, sending shockwaves of pleasure through her. He shifted slightly, leaning her against the sofa and trailed kisses along her jaw and neck while his hand skimmed her thigh. Max had forgotten how it felt to be desired by a man. Chris had awakened the part of her that had lain dormant for the past several years and she felt herself teetering on the brink of losing control.

Chris lifted his head and stroked a finger down her cheek. "There is something about you, something about your kisses that makes me forget that I want to take this slow."

With the way his kisses had set her body aflame, she wanted to tell him to forget slow and ask him to make love to her. Right. Now. She had no idea how he could've ever associated the word *rusty* with his kisses. Expert would be a better description.

"Did you have any plans for this afternoon?" he asked, still caressing her thigh and placing butterfly kisses on her face.

How in the hell does he expect me to answer with his hand and mouth on my body? "I...mmm. I had planned to go...walking at the park."

He sat up straight. "Want some company? It might be safer than being on this sofa."

Max gave him a sidelong glance. "Safe, maybe, but definitely not as much fun. And sure, I'd love the company. I just need to put on my shoes." She moved to stand and he came to his feet and helped her up. "Thanks. You get an A for being a gentleman."

Smiling, he kissed her forehead. "Doing my best."

"I'll be back in a minute." Once in her bedroom, she collapsed on the bed. Chris had told her he liked her. She smiled. *I like him, too.*

As soon as Max was out of sight, Chris dropped back down on the sofa, scrubbed a hand down his face and blew out a long breath. He hadn't meant for it to go that far, that fast. A few kisses and nothing too heavy, but as he'd told her, there was something about Max that made his control take a hike whenever he came near her.

For over a decade, he had steered clear of becoming emotionally involved after the woman he loved cheated with his now *former* best friend. Chris told himself, he should've known better. His parents had divorced when he was a teen and his sister's husband had walked out the moment he found out their premature daughter had been born with developmental delays. He'd seen very few relationships that lasted, and his liaisons were few and far between. None lasted more than a month or two. Now with Max, he felt differently and didn't know why. Every kiss they'd shared had stayed with him over the weekend and he found himself thinking about her all throughout his days and nights.

"Okay, I'm ready," Max said, coming around the corner.

Chris stood. She'd changed into another pair of those knit pants that spiked his arousal. They definitely needed to leave the house. Hopefully, by the time they returned, his body would have calmed down. "Where's the park?"

"A couple of miles away."

He dug his car keys out of his pocket. "I'll drive." He waited for her to lock the door, then led her out to his truck.

"No date car this time?" she teased.

"If I'd known we were going for a ride, I would've driven it." He helped her climb up and closed her door, then rounded the fender and got in on the driver's side.

Max glanced around. "I like this. My dad used to drive a Ford when I was growing up. Trucks have come a long way —all this luxury and technology, and a full backseat. I remember hating being all scrunched up in that small space."

He chuckled. "They have." Max's response to him driving a truck was completely different from some other women. One had refused to get in, telling him she couldn't be seen riding in a truck, and another had told him if he wanted to take her out, he needed to go home and get something more suitable. In both cases, he'd left them standing there and never looked back. The latter had tried calling him a couple of weeks later, but he refused to play those kind of games and blocked her number. "Which way?"

"End of the block and make a left. You'll run into it on the right."

It took less than five minutes to arrive. Apparently, they weren't the only ones taking advantage of the warmer fall weather. Chris saw several children on the playground and a few people on the walking trail. They joined them and started a brisk walk. "How often do you come here?"

"In the spring and early fall, at least three times a week. When it gets too cold, I do a workout from YouTube at home. What about you? Do you work out?"

"Same as you, but I have a gym setup at home."

Max glanced up at him. "Must be nice. I like weight training, but I hate going to the gym and having to wait until someone is done with a machine."

"That's exactly why I have my own." He liked getting in, doing his workout and getting out in an hour and that rarely happened. Most times, his muscles had cooled down before he could move on to the next exercise, reducing the benefits and wasting his money. They made a complete loop on the trail twice, then slowed their steps.

"We can head back now. Thanks for the company."

Chris reached for her hand. "I'll walk with you anytime you want." Especially since it meant spending more time with her.

"I'll keep that in mind." After a few minutes, she said, "I see the kids are still out here on the basketball court. I remember spending many days running behind my son when he played. Did you play any sports in high school?"

"Yep. I was one of those out on the basketball court. I still play with a few buddies in a recreational league."

"*Whaaat?* You'll have to let me know when you're playing, so I can come cheer you on. *Gooooo, Chris!*" She did a mock cheer, complete with the moves.

He threw his head back and roared with laughter. "Were you a cheerleader in high school?"

"Absolutely not. I was on that basketball court setting school records for most points in the game."

His stunned gaze met her amused one. "I think we might need to play a little one-on-one sometimes." He wiggled his eyebrows.

"I don't think so," she said with a chuckle. "I haven't played ball since I graduated high school thirty-five years ago."

Chris did a quick calculation in his head. "That would make you only fifty-three and not old." When she whipped her head in his direction, he smiled. "Hey, I didn't ask your age, you volunteered the information."

"Oh, whatever." Max playfully elbowed him and turned her head away briefly, but not before he saw her smile.

They shared a smile and he reclaimed her hand as they continued to stroll leisurely down the path in companionable silence. "Oh, I wanted to ask," he started after a few minutes, "about possibly changing the time on Friday. Since it gets dark earlier, would you mind us starting around five instead?"

"No. That should be fine. Is this going to be at your house or mine?"

He studied her. "Mine. Is there something wrong?"

She sighed. "It's nothing really wrong, but…"

Chris stopped walking and guided her over to a nearby bench. He sat and draped an arm around her shoulders. "Talk to me, Max."

"Have you told your sister about us?"

"Not yet, but I plan to talk to her tonight. Why?"

"It's just that she's a client and do you know how awkward it would be if this...this," she waved a hand, "thing between us crashes and burns? I have to come to *your* house *every week* probably for the next year or two."

He gave her a tender smile. "Sweetheart, I can't say what's going to happen in the future, only that I care about you. If this doesn't work out, we're two mature adults, and I'd like to think that we'd be able to handle it. I will promise that I'll never do anything to put you in an uncomfortable position as it relates to your job, even if it means me not being there on the days you come to see Malia. And you don't need to worry about Sandra. She'd probably take your side over mine in a heartbeat." Chris decided not to tell her that his sister already suspected he had feelings for Max. He tilted her chin and his gazed roamed over her beautiful face. "I want to be able to bring you to my home, but if you're uncomfortable, I can bring everything to your house. This time." The style of his home included a separate garage and entrance that had its own small living room leading to Sandra's bedroom suite. His room was on the opposite end with the formal living and dining rooms and kitchen between them. There was more than enough space for him to enjoy Max's company without his sister underfoot. Not that she would interrupt anyway, since her sole goal seemed to be finding him a wife.

Max didn't say anything for a moment, as if weighing her decision. Finally, she said, "Okay. I'll come to your house. You can pick me up any time after four-thirty."

He smiled and pressed a kiss to her lips, then stood and extended his hand. "Come on, baby."

Chris dropped Max off at home with a promise to call later and drove home.

His sister was sitting in the family room rocking Malia

when he arrived. He glanced down at his niece, who couldn't keep her eyes open and placed a light kiss on her forehead. He repeated the same action with Sandra. "Hey," he whispered.

"Hey, yourself. I don't think I've ever known you to be away from home this much," Sandra added with a smile.

He tweaked her nose. "That's because you don't know everything." He left her there and went into the kitchen to find something to eat, and was pleasantly surprised to see that she'd already made dinner. Chris went to his bedroom, took off his shoes and washed his hands. By the time he came back to the kitchen, Sandra was there fixing her plate.

"Thanks for dinner."

"You're letting me stay here rent-free. It's the least I can do." She took her plate to the bar and slid onto a stool. "Still waiting on the name of your mystery woman, and you never did say how the date went. Are you planning to see her again?"

Chris shook his head. She hadn't changed one bit. He brought his plate over and sat next to her. "I took Max to dinner."

Sandra let out a little squeal, then quickly covered her mouth. "*Yes!*" she whispered excitedly. "I really like Max, and I think you two will be good together."

"She'll be here for dinner on Friday."

She held up a hand. "Say no more. Malia and I will make ourselves scarce. What time is she coming over?"

He raised a brow. "I'm *picking her up* around four-thirty." He didn't care about having to make two round trips. In his book a date required him picking her up and dropping her off.

"My bad. Look at you being all chivalrous. I wish I had paid more attention to how you always treat women," she said wistfully. "Dad certainly wasn't a role model and maybe

I wouldn't be in this situation. You'd better believe I'm laser focused now, and if a brother steps to me, he's going to have to do all the things I see you do, or he needs to keep walking."

Chris bowed his head as his emotions surged. He'd always tried to be a good role model, but had no idea she'd watched him so closely. "That means a lot, sis."

Sandra laid a hand on his arm and smiled softly. "You have to know you're my superhero, Chris. It's time for at least one of us to find happiness. Promise me you won't let what happened with Janine keep you from being with Max."

He didn't have a reply, so he said nothing. The failure of his marriage was always in the back of his mind and admittedly, it had impacted his relationships. However, Chris couldn't recall the last time, if ever, he'd felt such contentment with a woman. Even the one he'd married. He hadn't allowed himself to get close to a woman, but the more time he spent with Max, the closer he wanted to be.

CHAPTER 6

*M*ax hugged her sister when she walked into the restaurant and over to the table Friday afternoon. "I'm so glad to see you. You look good, girl." She and Teresa looked enough alike for people to sometimes mistake them for twins, but Max stood an inch taller.

Teresa smiled. "So do you. I'm glad to be home." She claimed the chair across from Max. "Did you order yet?"

"Yes. I ordered chef salads."

"Great."

"Have you seen Mom and Dad yet?"

"I went by yesterday and had dinner. You would've thought I'd been gone for years instead of a few weeks the way Mom fussed over me."

She laughed. "Well, if you stopped gallivanting across the country, she wouldn't fuss so much. You know you're her baby."

"Whatever. She won't have a reason anymore because I've decided it's time to stay in one place. I have an interview with a doctor's office on Monday. I'm ready for some stable hours, preferably at a place that doesn't include weekends."

"Oh, Teresa, I'm so happy." Max had missed her tremendously and looked forward to being able to hang out with her more often now. The server returned with their salads and a basket filled with bread and butter.

"You wouldn't happen to know whether Nzinga has an opening in her pediatric practice?"

"No, but I'll give you her number and you can call and ask."

"That would be great. How are things with Dion?" she asked, starting in on her food. "I hope you've at least been able to talk with him. It still breaks my heart because I know how close you two used to be."

"He came by a couple of weeks ago and apologized."

Teresa's head came up sharply. "He did?"

Max nodded and smiled at the stunned look on her sister's face. It was the same she'd had. "Believe me, I was just as surprised. Apparently, Rolando finally married her and got caught in his own lies." She shared the details of her conversation with Dion and how angry her son had been. "I felt so bad for my baby, and I wanted to go over and knock the hell out of Rolando for what he put Dion through."

She shook her head in disgust. "It would serve him right, the arrogant bastard. You tried to tell him not to involve Dion, but he just wouldn't listen. Now, it's come back to bite him in the ass. My poor nephew."

"Exactly." Every time Max thought about the time she lost with her son, all the important moments, she got angry all over again. She ate a forkful of her salad. After a few minutes, she said, "I met someone."

Teresa's eyes lit up. "Are you *serious*? That's fantastic, Max. Okay, I need all the details—name, age, height, how you met, what he looks like. How are his kisses and can he bring it in the bedroom?"

"I think you're getting to be more outrageous than me," she said with a chuckle. "His name is Chris and he's the uncle of one of my clients." She gave a rundown of their first encounter, his subsequent apology and their dinner date."

"Aw, I love it. But you skipped a few things, dear sister," Teresa said, a smile playing around the corner of her mouth.

"I don't know what you mean," Max said innocently as she sipped her water.

"Mmm hmm. Liar. You know *exactly* what I mean. I want to know the juicy stuff, so spill it."

Max couldn't hide her smile. "He told me that he hadn't kissed a woman in a while and was rusty. But honey, there wasn't one speck of *rust* in his kisses. They were more like a five-alarm blaze."

"*Dayum!*" The word came out in three syllables. She picked up her glass of water and drained the contents, then fanned herself. If I had known we'd be having this kind of conversation, I would've ordered something a lot stronger than water. And in the bedroom?"

"I have no idea." But she'd be lying if she said she hadn't thought about it. If the way he kissed and touched her was any indication, she didn't think he'd have any problems in the bedroom.

"Girl, you have to try out the goods. You don't want to waste time on a man who sucks where it counts. I bet the other sassy sisters would agree with me."

Max pointed her fork in Teresa's direction. "See, that's exactly why you can't roll with us."

Teresa brought a hand to her chest, as if offended. "What? I've got plenty of sass."

"But not enough *seasoning*." They dissolved in a fit of laughter. Once calm, she said, "Seriously though, I like that he's not trying to rush things. Don't get me wrong, I can tell he's attracted to me, but I appreciate the slower pace for a change. I'm not saying how long it'll last, though. There's only so much a sister can take."

"Now *that's* the big sister I know."

She glanced at her watch. "It's almost time for me to leave, and messing around with you I've eaten less than half my food."

"Just wrap it up and have the rest for dinner. That's what I plan to do."

"I'm having dinner with Chris tonight. He's cooking…at his place."

"Cooking for you on a second date? Oh, hell yeah. I need to meet this brother. He sounds like a keeper." Teresa waved a server over and requested boxes.

"It's been less than a month, so the jury is still out." But as crazy as it sounded, she could see herself with him long-term. She enjoyed the way they could talk about everything and nothing, didn't need to fill every moment with conversation, and how he made her smile. The kisses were a definite bonus. After boxing up their leftovers, Max overruled her sister and paid the bill. They spoke a moment longer in the parking lot, then went their separate ways.

In her car, Max checked her emails and messages and saw that her last appointment had canceled. Had she known earlier, she could have spent a little longer with Teresa. "Oh, well," she said aloud and headed home.

She had been home an hour when she received a text message from Donna in their group chat: *We need to find out what's going on with this new guy.* A Zoom link followed. Max loved her girls. She grabbed her laptop and powered it on. She'd told Chris he could pick her up any time after four-thirty, so she still had a good half hour to chat with her friends. With her Sassy Seasoned Sister cup filled with water, she settled in front of the screen.

"Hey, girl," Donna said.

"Hey. You know you're crazy, right?" Before Donna could reply, Nzinga and Val popped up on the screen. She greeted them both.

"Okay, let's hear it," Nzinga said. "Val said there were some hot kisses going on."

Val laughed. "Yeah, I want to know if his kisses have improved any."

"He doesn't need to improve because those kisses are damn near perfect and had me *weak*," Max said. The three women screamed. "And the way his hands moved…"

"I know you're bringing him next week," Val said.

"I forgot to ask, but I will when he gets here today."

Nzinga lifted a brow. "Today? You have a date with him today?"

She nodded.

"The brother started out with Morton's, so I don't know where he can go from there," Donna chimed in.

"He's cooking for me. At his house." She told them about being a little uncomfortable because his sister's a client. "I mean, what if it doesn't work out? I don't want to run into him every week."

"I hear you," Nzinga said. "But what if it does? How old is he?"

Max hesitated. "He's a little younger."

Val snapped her fingers. "Aw, sookie, sookie. My girl is out here being a cougar."

"He'll be fifty in a few months. That hardly qualifies as me being a cougar, crazy woman." Chris appeared to be far more mature than the last two guys she'd dated, and he didn't play head games. He tended to be direct and straight to the point. Just like her.

"I can't wait to meet him," Donna said. "So you'd better not forget to ask him about the dance."

"I won't. Oh, you're not going to believe what happened. I've been so busy, I forgot to tell y'all Dion came over and apologized."

"Sis, that is wonderful. I know Monique will be glad. Every time I talk to her, she asks if he's come to his senses yet."

"Donna, you can tell my goddaughter he's no longer acting like a butthead," she said with a laugh. "It seems he finally found out his father had been lying to him this whole time." She opened her mouth to say something else and heard her doorbell. "I'll have to tell you the rest later. I think Chris is at the door."

"Tell him we said hello and we can't wait to meet him," Nzinga said.

"More like interrogate him," Donna added.

"I love y'all. Bye." Max hit the Leave Meeting button and went to answer the door.

Her smile faded when she saw Rolando standing on her porch and not Chris. She heaved a deep sigh. *I don't have time for his bullshit today.* She snatched the door open. "What can I do for you, Rolando?"

"Can I come in? I need to talk to you," Rolando said tightly.

She contemplated slamming the door in his face. Inviting evil and drama into her home wasn't something she liked doing.

"Max?"

She unlocked the screen and stepped back. He came in and she stood there with her arms folded, waiting. Max didn't offer him a seat because she didn't plan for him to stay long enough to get comfortable. "What do you want?"

"What did you tell my son?"

"I haven't told him anything. Why?"

"He won't answer my calls."

"Hmph. Sort of like how he's done me for the past six years. Isn't that something?" She didn't know what she ever saw in him.

"Cut the crap, Max. I know you said something."

Her anger flared. "Crap? You're the only one who's full of crap. You have a lot of nerve bringing your ass to my house after all the shit you've put me through. You lied and cost me *six* damn years with my son, and now that you've gotten caught, you want to come over here acting like you don't know why."

"For you not saying anything, you sure know a lot," he snapped.

She pointed her finger in his face. "I didn't have to say anything. You did that yourself. Karma's a *bitch* and I told you all your lies were going to catch up to you one day. I'm just glad I'm around to see it." The alternating knocking on her door and the ringing doorbell interrupted her tirade. *Chris. Just great.*

Chris heard the loud voices halfway up the walkway, but it was the angry male voice that had his heart pumping. It took everything inside him not to just barge in. It brought back memories of his parents' constant arguing and his father hitting his mother. As a kid, he couldn't do anything to stop it, but he was a grown man now and he'd be damned if he'd let something happen to Max.

"Hey, Chris." Max held the door open.

"Are you okay?" He scanned her face. "I heard yelling."

"Yeah, I'm fine. Just clearing the air with my ex."

Her ex? Inside, he saw a man standing in the middle of

living room with his hands resting on his hips, and clearly angry. Max didn't make any introductions and that suited Chris just fine. He didn't need to know the man's name. The only thing on his mind was Max's safety.

"He's just leaving." Max stalked back over to the door and pointed. "Get out of my house."

The man glared at Max and stormed across the room. As he walked out the door, he turned back. "You've always been a bi—"

Chris took a step. Before he could utter a word, Max hauled off and punched the man in his face, sending him sprawling and tumbling down the steps.

"Don't you *ever* call me out my name or bring your ass to my house again," she said through clenched teeth.

She started out the door and Chris lifted her off her feet, brought her back into the house and kissed her temple. "It's okay, baby. I've got this." He went to the man still clutching his jaw and trying to get up from the pavement, leaned down and said with lethal calmness, "You only get this one warning." He climbed the steps, gave him one last warning glare before going inside, and slamming the door. Taking a couple of deep breaths, he reined in his fury. He gathered Max in his embrace. "Are you sure you're okay?"

"I'm fine now. I've been wanting to knock him on his ass since I caught him screwing that heifer in my bed. He lied and told our son I was the one who cheated. Dion believed him and our relationship was nearly non-existent for six years. He's just mad now because Dion found out the truth and he wants to blame me. I've finally got my son back and I'll be damned if I let him screw it up."

The tears in her eyes incensed him all over again. "Not if he knows what's good for him. I won't let him hurt you ever again." The last sentence had slipped out. But as soon as he said it, Chris knew he meant every word. He sat on the sofa, pulled her down onto his lap and just held her for a while.

"Thank you."

"No thanks necessary." He couldn't believe the man had cheated on a woman like her. "You said he cheated with someone in your bed?"

Max lifted her head from his chest. "Yes. My three friends and I had gone to Napa for the weekend, sort of a girls trip. But Nzinga got sick and we came back a day early. They were so busy, they didn't notice me. I took a few pictures and a video, left and went to spend the night at a hotel. The next day, I called Val, who's an attorney, and filed for divorce. Have you ever been married?"

"For about forty-five minutes."

Her eyes widened. "What?"

"We'd been at the reception for about twenty minutes and she went off with her maid of honor for some reason or another. They were about to serve dinner, and when she didn't come back after a few minutes, I went looking for her. I found my brand new wife and my best friend having sex."

"Just. Wow." Max shook her head. "That's really crazy. I'm so sorry."

"Yeah. Fortunately, the minister was still there. I had him follow me back to the room where they were still going at it. I don't know what shocked him more, them or me asking for the marriage license. But he gave it to me and I ripped it in half and left." What he didn't say was that he'd confronted them both and pretty much did the same thing she'd just done to her ex-husband. The only difference was that when Chris walked out of the hotel, ignoring Janine's pleas for forgiveness, the man he'd called friend all his life was still lying on the floor unconscious.

"After all that food and cake tasting, I would've been pissed."

Chris chuckled. Leave it to Max to find some humor.

"At least you didn't waste eighteen years of your life and have to worry about going through a nasty divorce." She waved a hand. "Okay, I'm done talking about ignorant folks."

"What do you want to talk about?"

"Nothing. I—"

"Me, either," he said, cutting her off and slanting his mouth over hers, inhaling her words. Just like every other kiss they'd shared, her unique sweetness filled him with a pleasure he'd never experienced. She met him stroke for stroke, her tongue tangling and dancing with his, sending a raging fire through his body. If he had any hope of them getting that dinner, he needed to end the kiss. *Now*. Yet, he couldn't stop. Didn't want to stop. His hands roamed down her back and over her hips, and he pulled her soft curves closer to the fit of his body. She moaned and the soft sound spiked his arousal. Chris wanted nothing more than to make love to her, but he'd promised to cook her dinner and something inside him said it wasn't the right time. He finally forced himself to end the kiss. "These lips of yours are going to get us into trouble."

Max smiled and said sensually, "Not all trouble is bad, and didn't you say you weren't opposed to indulging in a sweet, delectable dessert every now and again?"

Chris shot to his feet with Max in his arms and set her down and away from him. "It's time for us to get out of here."

Her sweet laughter filled the room. "I'll be back in a minute."

He used the few minutes she was gone to bring his body back under control. The woman was temptation personified and he wondered how long he would last before surrendering to what he knew would be an explosive passion. She returned wearing a pair of snug jeans and a V-neck top that emphasized her full breasts, further spiking his arousal. *Yeah, we need to leave.*

"Alright, I'm ready to go sample this five-star dinner." Once in the car, Max asked, "What are we having with it?"

"I thought I'd keep it simple and do some roasted red potatoes and sautéed broccoli and mushrooms."

"I can't wait. Oh, I've been meaning to ask you something. Do you have any plans for next Saturday?"

"No, but I was hoping to spend the day with you—maybe go out to lunch. Why?"

"My class reunion committee is throwing a dinner and dance—it's dressy—and I'd like you to be my date."

"Are you asking me out on a date, Ms. Richardson?" he asked, throwing back the same words she said to him that first time.

She smiled over at him and batted her eyelashes. "Yes, and I promise to be on my *very* best behavior."

Chris laughed so hard, he thought he would have to pull over. "I would absolutely love to be your date."

"If you want to still have lunch, that's fine. I had planned to go to Scentillating Touch in Old Sac, but I can go another time."

"If you don't mind the company, I'll take you and we can have lunch afterward."

"Sounds like a plan. Why don't you just bring what you plan to wear and you can change at my house. That'll save you a trip and some gas."

The thought of them changing clothes in the same house at the same time gave him momentary pause. He wasn't sure he could handle knowing she'd be damn near naked in another room. His eyes left the road briefly and he found her staring at him, waiting. "That works." He thought it ironic that they lived in the same city, less than five miles apart, and had never run into each other. If he had, he would have definitely remembered. Maxine Richardson wasn't a woman a man could easily forget. When he got home, he parked in the driveway and let them in through the front door.

"I really like your home. How many bedrooms do you have?"

Chris gave her a strange look, then it dawned on him that her presence in his house had always been for business and she hadn't ventured past the family room where she conducted her session. "Four bedrooms and four and a half baths. I'll give you a tour once I get everything started." He noticed the uncomfortable expression on her face and sought to reassure her. He grasped her hands. "Max, tonight, we're two people who enjoy each other's company, nothing more. Put any thoughts of work out of your mind and relax. I want you to have a good time."

"I'll do my best." She came up on tiptoe and gave him a quick kiss. "How can I help?"

He stared at her incredulously. "You can't. The only thing you get to do is sit, sip a glass of wine or whatever you'd like to drink and enjoy yourself." She stared at him strangely. "What?"

"You're so different," Max said softly.

"Good or bad?"

"Very good."

He smiled. "I'll take it." Unable to resist, he lowered his head and kissed her softly. "Come. You can tell me what you'd like to drink." After settling Max with a glass of wine on his back deck, Chris started dinner. It would be the first time he actually prepared a meal for a woman. Janine had preferred going out and being the life of the party rather than have a quiet evening at home, something that should have given him a clue she wasn't who she'd led him to believe.

He'd purchased the house fifteen years ago, intending to live in it with his wife and any children they had. But Janine hadn't spent one night under its roof. Aside from his sister and mother, Max was the only woman to cross the threshold and he had to wonder if it was some kind of sign. Once the meat was on the grill, he walked over to the lounger where Max sat and extended his hand. "Ready for the tour?"

"Yep."

She'd already seen the living and family rooms, and kitchen, so he started with the two guest bedrooms that had been minimally furnished with full-sized beds, dressers and nightstands. Each one had its own bath. He skipped the dining room because that's where they would eat. He'd originally planned for them to eat outside, but when Sandra found out, she nearly took his head off. She'd told him Max was a lady, and he needed to treat her like one and set the dining table with his best china, silver, candles and flowers. After she'd helped him lay everything out, he had to admit her idea had been far better than his.

"This is so gorgeous. I really like the layout."

"Thanks." Chris gestured her into the master bedroom.

"Now this is what I call a master retreat."

He watched as Max walked around the spacious room that had a sitting area holding two chaise loungers and a small table, fireplace and a balcony leading to the backyard.

"Is that a tool shed? It looks more like a small house."

"My home gym." Her mouth formed the perfect 'O' and he laughed. "I had the patio cover extended for when it rains." He slid the glass door open and followed her out. He'd purchased a treadmill, bench press, and set of dumbbells, which suited his workout needs perfectly.

"You have everything here. No wonder you don't go to the gym. I wouldn't either, if I had this setup."

"You're welcome to use it whenever you like," he said, smiling.

"Hmm," was all Max said as she went back inside.

"Let me show you the other side of the house real quick, so I can get back to the grill. Can't serve you a burnt steak."

"Now that's a sure way for you to get yourself back into that ditch," she said laughingly.

"Yeah, not jumping in there again." Chris escorted her down the hallway and through the living room to another small area that doubled as a second family room.

"Now this is cool. Is this where you enter from the one-car garage?"

He nodded. "Sandra parks in there and she has the other master bedroom through that hallway. It's a little smaller, but has a sitting area set up for Malia."

"Oops."

They both turned when Sandra appeared.

"Don't mind me. I just need to get something out of my car. Hi, Max. Enjoy yourself. Bye, Max." Sandra skirted past them and went out the door, but not before she gave Chris the thumbs up.

He and Max chuckled, and she followed him back out to the deck. Thirty minutes later, they sat down to eat.

"Oh, my goodness. This looks *so* good. You didn't say anything about shrimp. And this table setting is better than the one at the restaurant. I'm impressed."

Thanks, sis, he said silently. Chris had topped their steaks with an herbed butter and the grilled shrimp. "I hope it tastes as good." He waited until she took her first bites before picking up his knife and fork.

Max let out a soft moan and placed a hand on his arm. "Listen, if you can cook like this, you don't ever have to spend money at a restaurant again. You can cook for me *forever*."

Forever? The word sent a sliver of fear down his spine. Forever never seemed to work for him, but as he studied Max's smiling face, something stirred in his heart and he was forced to acknowledge that he had fallen for this gorgeous woman. He could only hope that this time would be different.

CHAPTER 7

"Hey, baby," Chris said, entering Max's house Saturday afternoon.

Max tilted her head to receive the kiss she'd been craving all week. She'd only seen him briefly while at his house during his niece's therapy session. Although, she had been the one who wanted to keep the lines between personal and professional separate, she'd been secretly disappointed that he hadn't walked her out or given any outward signs that they were involved. "Follow me. You can put your bag in the second bedroom."

"Is there anywhere in particular you'd like to go for lunch?" he asked as they left the bedroom and headed out.

"Not really, but I'm thinking I want something light, since there will be food tonight." It was already after one and the dinner started at seven, with a cocktail hour at six.

"We can walk around Old Sac after you finish shopping and see what's there. If we don't find anything, we'll go somewhere else."

"Okay." While he drove, Max thought about where she wanted this relationship to go. Even though they'd only been dating about a month, she had finally admitted to herself that she was falling hard for Chris. How could she not fall for a man who brought her roses, cooked for her and kissed like he created the art? How he'd held her after the mess with Rolando had pushed her emotions over the top. That and his assurance that he'd be there for her. No man, other than her father, had made her feel so safe. Her mind went back to their dinner and she smiled. It had been the best steak she had ever eaten, hands down. She couldn't keep from wondering how many other women had he cooked for, even though it shouldn't matter. They were both adults with pasts. Max was still shocked by the fact that he'd walked in on his wife with another man at their wedding reception. *She and Rolando would be perfect for each other*, she thought sarcastically. The sultry wail of a saxophone drew her out of her thoughts. The mid-tempo jazz piece had a Latin flair and totally drew her in. "I love this." Apparently, Chris did, too, because he tapped his fingers on his thigh in time with the beat.

"It's nice. You like Jackiem Joyner?"

"I do now." She glanced at the digital display and had to chuckle inwardly at the title: "Beautiful Seduction." *Figures.* She made a mental note to download some of his music.

"Do you want me to park in the garage or try to find parking near the shop?"

Max surveyed the streets. "It doesn't look too crowded, so we can see if there's something on the streets." She directed him to where the store was located and he found a spot less than a block away. Chris held her hand as they headed toward the bath and body store that had a variety of handmade products.

"I've never been here," Chris said when they entered.

"Most men don't, but she has a nice selection of men's soaps, shower gels and lotions."

"Hmm, maybe I'll check them out."

"Hi, I'm Desiree. Welcome to Scentillating Touch. Is there anything in particular I can help you find?"

Max returned the woman's warm smile. "You're the owner, right?"

"I am," Desiree said proudly.

"I love your bath bombs and hand scrubs, and…everything," she said with a laugh. "I get into a lot of trouble every time I come in here to replenish my "me time" stash. I need more of the hand scrub and a few bath bombs." The bath bombs were perfect for her monthly "me time" ritual, which included a long bath with candles and soft music.

"We also have some things that are perfect for couples." Desiree pointed to a shelf containing massage oils and body paints. She retrieved a small bottle. "This is an edible, warming massage oil. You can put it anywhere," she added with a wink.

Chris chuckled. "Interesting."

"I can guarantee it works." She cradled her rounded belly. "*Trust me.*"

He stared down at Max with that *look* that always turned her on and she felt her cheeks warm. "Um…I'll just be over near the hand scrubs." Max never ran from anything, but she thought it best that she step away from that shelf so she wouldn't be tempted to purchase every flavor of that oil. Several minutes later, Chris came over to where she stood trying to decide which fragrance of bath bombs she wanted.

"Still looking?" he asked.

"I can't decide which ones to get. They all smell so good." She pointed at the small bag in his hand. "I see you didn't have any trouble."

He held it up. "You were right. I bought a couple bars of soap and Desiree helped me pick out something for my sister."

"Aw, you're so sweet. Okay, I'm getting these three. I've already got the scrub and hand cream." He eased the scrub from her hand and read the label. "Between the hand sanitizer and washing my hands so much, I need something to keep them soft."

Chris reached for her hand and brushed his lips across the back, then turned it over and repeated the gesture on her palm, his eyes never leaving hers. *Please don't let me swoon in this store.* Her breathing increased and warmth spread through her. "Chris," she whispered.

"I agree. They're very soft." He placed one more lingering kiss on her palm, then released her hand. "Pick out what you want and I'll take care of it."

It took a moment for the sensual haze to clear and his words to register. "Wait. What? Oh, you don't have to buy these for me."

A smile touched his lips. "I want to buy them for you."

She opened her mouth to protest and he cut it off with a kiss.

"Get what you want, sweetheart. I've got this."

The endearment went straight to her heart and she fell a little harder. Max managed a nod, made her selections and followed him to the register where he whipped out his credit card before she could blink. "Thank you," she said as he handed her the bag.

"You're welcome."

They walked back to the car to leave the packages, then strolled around in search of food. In the end, they stopped at a deli and took everything to a park. By the time he parked in her driveway, they only had an hour to shower and change before leaving for the dinner.

Max slipped into the one-shoulder wine-colored dress that stopped mid-calf, hugged her curves and had a generous front slit that ended a few inches above her knees. The black strappy sandals added four-inches to her height and she didn't have to worry about being taller than her date. Grabbing her purse and wrap, she took one last look at her reflection. Her stomach wasn't as flat as she wanted, but she'd earned every dip, wrinkle and curve, so she didn't stress herself about it. Max turned one way, then another. Pleased with her look, she turned off all the lights, except the nightstand lamp and headed down the hall to the living room.

Chris rose to his feet when she walked into the room. "You look absolutely stunning. I'm honored to be the man by your side tonight."

"Thank you. You look good, too. I hope I don't have to act up tonight if some woman tries to come on to my man."

He smiled, then he turned serious. "Am I your man, Max?"

"Yes."

"That's good because you are definitely my woman. And for the record, I protect what's mine. I hope *I* don't have to act up."

She laughed. "Let's go." The thirty-minute drive was completed in silence interspersed with quiet conversation.

Chris turned the car over to the hotel's valet and escorted Max inside. "Do you keep in contact with the people from your class?"

"I have three best friends who are like sisters and we've been together since sixth grade. They can't wait to meet you."

He chuckled. "Should I be worried?"

"Nah, I only told them the good stuff." Max made a show of thinking. "Well, on second thought… I'm just kidding." She knew for a fact that her friends would like him.

"Well, if it isn't the fourth member of the Musketeers. I wondered where you were."

Max whirled around. "Hey, Lamont." She hugged him. "You know I wasn't missing this shindig, especially since my favorite jazz band is playing." She reached for Chris' hand. "Chris this is Lamont Johnson. Lamont, Chris." The two men exchanged greetings and handshakes. "Lamont is the jazz band's keyboardist and leader."

"I'm a jazz man and I'm looking forward to some good music."

"Have you seen my girls?" Max asked.

"They're all here and were sitting on the left side of the stage near the front. You know we had to make sure y'all got good seats."

"Thanks, Lamont. See you later." She and Chris entered the large ballroom and she waved at some people she knew, but didn't stop to talk. When she spotted her three friends, they jumped up from their seats and rushed over.

"Hey, girl. Ooh, you look good. That man is *fine*!" Val whispered, hugging Max.

"So do you." Because she'd be on the drum set, Val had worn a stylish pantsuit. She hugged Nzinga and Donna. "Chris, I want you to meet my sisters of the heart, Valina Anderson—attorney and drummer extraordinaire, Donna Harper—the best private investigator in the business, and Nzinga Walker—pediatrician and newlywed."

"It's a pleasure to meet you ladies."

Nzinga smiled. "It's nice to finally meet you. We've heard a lot about you."

"Hopefully, only good things."

"*All* good," Val said.

Donna shook her head and smiled. "Nice meeting you, Chris."

"Chris, this is my husband, Byron," Nzinga said, reaching for Byron's hand.

"It's good to meet you, Chris. I have to warn you, these four women are a trip. They still giggle like they're teenagers when they get together. They aren't called the *Sassy Seasoned Sisters* for nothing."

"Hush, Byron." Max playfully elbowed him. She looked up at Chris. "Don't believe a word he says. And that name was given to us by our goddaughter."

Chris grinned. "I'll reserve judgement for later."

"I'm on my way to get Nzinga a drink," Byron said. "You can come with me and I'll give you the lowdown."

He kissed Max's temple. "Sounds like a plan. What can I get you, baby?"

"A glass of white wine, please." She watched him and Byron cross the room. Their height and sexy swagger had just about every woman in the room staring.

Val moved closer to Max. "Max, you're lucky you're my girl. Otherwise, I might have to push you to the side and go after that man."

They all laughed.

"Is he as nice as he seems?"

"Yeah, Donna, he is," she answered, still staring his way.

Nzinga chuckled. "Mmm hmm, and I bet he has you thinking about a hot night of sex."

Max laughed. She'd said the same thing to Nzinga after her first date with Byron. "Yes, but unlike you, I plan to do something about it." The women fell out laughing, drawing stares from nearby tables.

"Uh oh," Nzinga said. "Max, I think you're going to need that I-don't-like-you sign. Greg Hilton is heading this way fast."

She groaned. She'd danced with him once during the class reunion and the man had followed her around for the rest of the evening trying to convince her to give him her phone number. He'd fancied himself in love with her during high school and had asked her to every single dance, including homecoming and the junior and senior proms.

"Well hello, ladies," Greg said as soon as he got close to the table. "Maxine, Maxine, you sure are looking good tonight." He did a not-so-subtle glimpse down at her left hand. "I see you're still not married."

"Not yet," Chris said from behind and slid a possessive arm around her waist. "Here's your wine, baby."

"Thanks, love." She leaned up and kissed him.

Greg divided a glance between the two. "Baby?"

Chris took a step. "Yes. And you are?"

With Chris towering over Greg by a good eight or nine inches, Greg obviously decided Max wasn't worth the trouble because he beat a hasty retreat. Max shook her head. "I still can't stand him."

"Is this what I have to look forward to all night—fending off would-be suitors?"

"Probably," Byron said with a chuckle. "Most of them are harmless, though."

"No," Max countered. "But I did notice far more women staring at you and Byron. And I do have my Vaseline in my purse." Everyone at the table broke out in laughter. "Chris, I'll just need you to make sure we don't get arrested."

Still laughing, Chris threw his hands up in mock surrender. "Hey, I'm off duty, and I protect the *highways*, not ballroom brawls."

Max hooked her arm in Chris'. "Aw, come on, baby. I'll make it worth your while." She'd been teasing, but the flash of desire that immediately lit his eyes told her she was playing with fire and his words confirmed it.

He leaned over and whispered, "Max, don't tempt me. I'll throw you over my shoulder and have you out of here and upstairs in one of these hotel rooms before you can blink. And *I'll* make sure *every single minute* is worth *your* while."

Her pulse skipped. She snatched up her wine and took a hasty gulp.

Donna, sitting on the other side of Max, leaned close and started humming Nelly's "Hot In Here."

Obviously, Nzinga and Val heard her because both were biting their lips and struggling not to laugh. Max didn't know what shocked her the most, his words or the fact that she was tempted to stand and tell him to *bring it on*.

After dinner ended, Chris sat at the table waiting for Max to return and sipped the remainder of his water. At the moment he needed something much stronger. He'd known she had been teasing with her earlier comment, but every intimate touch or caress had pushed him to make the bold statement. And he'd been dead serious. She'd only have to say the word for him to make good on his promise.

He spotted her entering the ballroom and his gaze was riveted to the sexy sway of her hips and flash of her bare leg through that slit with every step. From the day he'd met her, she had ignited a steadily growing flame within him without even trying. But by just being her beautiful, outrageous self. He made her want to reach for love again, to let go of his fear of relationship failures. Chris didn't know if he could, but for her, he would give it his best shot.

"You look like you could use this." Byron sat a glass filled with an amber liquid in front of Chris.

"Thanks. You read my mind." He took a sip of what he recognized was whiskey and Coke, his eyes still on Max as one person after another stopped her. The enchanting smile, sparkling dark brown eyes and curvaceous body had him completely mesmerized. She laughed at whatever the person she was talking to said and, though he sat on the other side of the room, he could still hear the melodious and infectious sound in his head. Byron's low chuckle drew him out of his musings.

"Man, you've got it bad. How long have you and Max been together?"

"A little over a month. She's my niece's therapist. And the first time I saw her, I felt like I'd been hit by a tsunami."

"An intelligent and beautiful woman can do that to you."

Chris tore his gaze away from Max and shifted his attention to Byron. "Max mentioned you and Nzinga are newlyweds. Congratulations. How long have you known her?"

A smile curved Byron's mouth and he briefly glanced at his wife before turning back to Chris. "I went to school with her. Technically, she was my freshman brother's study partner. I fell for her on sight, but being three years older and a senior, her parents nipped our relationship in the bud before it got started. It was tough, but I respected their wishes," he added with a shrug. "I hadn't seen her in thirty-five years and happened to visit my brother the weekend of their class reunion this past summer. I took one look at her and knew I still loved her. And when I found out she was divorced, I had no intentions of letting her get away again."

He heard the deep affection in Byron's voice and could count on one hand the number of couples he knew who had the same kind of love. He wasn't one of them and had decided long ago that some things weren't meant for everyone. Chris had been fine with it…until Max. "My track record with relationships hasn't been all that great." He usually didn't share his private life with anyone, and didn't know why he'd blurted it out to Byron.

"Mine wasn't either until Nzinga came back into my life. I'm going to give you a little free advice. If you care about Max, you need to do everything in your power to keep her. Don't let what happened in your past rob you of having the right woman in your life. Max is beautiful and special, and if you don't want her, I guarantee there will be a line of men ready to step in and take your place."

Chris narrowed his eyes at one of those men who happened to be holding Max's hand longer than politeness dictated. He drained the rest of the contents in his glass and set it down with a thud. "I couldn't agree more. I'm going to get my woman." He stood and strode across the room.

"Would you like to dance, Max?" Chris heard the man ask.

Chris glowered at the man, who had yet to let go of her hand. He slid his arm around Max's waist and pulled her closer to him. "Max's first dance belongs to me." The man opened his mouth to protest, but Chris wasn't hearing it. Instead, he pressed a kiss to her temple. "Ready to hit the dance floor, baby?"

"Absolutely. Nice seeing you again." As soon as they were a few steps away, Max said, "Thanks for the rescue. I was trying not to make a scene."

"You weren't the only one," he muttered and guided her out onto the dance floor. The music changed to a ballad and he gathered her in his embrace, swaying slowly in time with the beat. She felt so good in his arms, as if she belonged there, and Chris felt a sense of completeness unlike anything he'd ever known. Once again, thoughts of his past crept into his mind. He pushed them aside and concentrated on the woman he held against his heart. His hands made an unhurried path down her back and he drew her closer to the fit of his body. And she did fit. Perfectly.

She nuzzled her nose against his throat. "You smell so good."

He chuckled. "And you smell good enough to eat."

She lifted her head and stared at him. "Like one of those sweet, decadent desserts?"

Chris slowly shook his head. "No. Something much better." Unable to resist, he touched his lips to hers. The song ended and Lakeside's "Something About That Woman" blared through the speakers.

Max threw her hands in the air. "Yes! This is my *song*." She spun around, presenting him with her rounded backside, and did a hip swivel and dip.

His breath caught and he nearly stumbled. He swore under his breath as arousal hit him hard and fast. It took him a moment to recover and find his rhythm. Perspiration dotted his brow and he couldn't take his eyes off her dancing with reckless abandon. Something told him she'd bring that same spirit to the bedroom, and he felt his plan to take things at a leisurely pace crumbling. It was all he could do not to carry out the promise he'd whispered in her ear. Chris had never been so glad for a song to end, and he knew from now on, he'd never be able to hear the song without thinking of her. The song title fit her perfectly because there was definitely something about Ms. Maxine Richardson that affected him like no other woman.

"Whew, that was fun," Max said, fanning herself as he led her off the dance floor.

"You ain't nothing nice, girl. You're about two seconds from becoming my dessert. Here and *now*."

She smiled, stepped back and eyed him from head to toe. "Hmm...that could be...tricky. But I'm willing if you are." She tossed him a bold wink and strutted off toward their table.

Chris stood there with his mouth hanging open for several seconds before catching up with her. He didn't have an opportunity to reply, as someone stepped onto the stage and called for everyone's attention.

"I do hope you all are having a great time. A big thank you to Vibes & Rhythm for getting the party started in the best way," the woman said. Thunderous applause and whistles sounded throughout the room and she had to wait until the noise died down so she could continue. "We're going to keep the party going with our own alumni jazz band. Okay my people, let's get ready to jam! You might want to take this time to refresh your drinks and yourselves because, *trust me*, you aren't going to want to miss one second of this performance."

"Alright, Val. I saw Desmond earlier. Go on up there and remind him, once again, why you'll always be the reigning percussion queen, my sister." Max and Val exchanged a high five.

Val stood and laughed. "He already asked if I'd let him play one of the songs and I ignored his behind. Just like when we were in school, he always wanted to be in the spotlight, but never brought his trifling butt to practice."

Donna rolled her eyes. "Boy, bye."

"Looks like he's still trying to plead his case." Nzinga gestured toward the stage. "Aw, and the answer is still no." They all watched the man stalk away with a frown.

Byron chuckled. "You ladies haven't changed one bit." He looked over at Chris. "Chris, this is mild. You should see when they really start acting up."

Nzinga elbowed Byron. "Oh, be quiet. Don't listen to him, Chris."

Chris smiled. "Maybe I should've attended my high school reunion activities. I had no idea I was missing all this drama."

"Don't start no drama, won't be no drama," Val said, flipping her sticks in her hand as she sauntered off.

"See, I told you," Byron said.

Chris couldn't remember the last time he'd enjoyed an evening. He'd rarely seen the kind of friendship Max shared with the three ladies, and he'd found them all to be as beautiful on the inside as they were on the outside. All eyes turned to the stage when the band struck the first note. Halfway through the first song, he understood what the announcer meant. The band was phenomenal, and he had to agree with Max's assessment. Val never had to worry about being dethroned. They had everyone on their feet as they played everything from Earth, Wind & Fire and Con Funk Shun, to Michael Jackson, Lakeside and The Isley Brothers. When the night finally ended, many people stood around talking and exchanging information. Chris stood outside the ballroom with Byron, waiting for Max, Val, Nzinga and Donna to return from the ladies room. The two men made plans to get together for a basketball game.

A woman approached, smiling flirtatiously. "You two look like you could use a little company. The party doesn't have to end. My friend and I would love to have you over for an *after* party. Why don't you introduce me to your friend, Byron." She tried to hook her arm in Byron's, but he quickly stepped back.

"Darlene," Byron said. "My *wife* is all the company I need."

"Wife?" she said, her eyes widening. "I saw you at the picnic five months ago and you weren't even dating anyone. Now you expect me to believe you met, dated and married somebody since then."

"I don't care what you believe."

Up to that point, Byron hadn't made any introductions, which suited Chris just fine. With her cloying perfume, overly made-up face and revealing dress, she never would have made the list of women he'd choose to date.

"Ready, honey?" Nzinga said as she walked up and slid her arm around Byron's waist.

Chris chuckled inwardly at the death glare Nzinga shot the woman, the glare all four friends were giving the woman. "Ready, sweetheart?" he asked Max, reaching for her hand.

Darlene looked Chris up and down and said to Max, "He's with *you?*"

He felt Max stiffen and thought it a good time to make

their exit. "It was nice meeting you all. Byron, I'll be in touch."

"Oh, we're all leaving," Donna said. "Have a good evening, Darlene."

As soon as they got outside, Val said, "One of these days, somebody is going to knock Darlene on her ass, always trying to make a play for men she clearly knows are taken."

"I know that's right," Max muttered.

They handed their valet tickets off and waited for the cars to be brought around. Chris' was the first out. He waited while Max hugged her friends, then helped her into the car.

"Thanks for coming along as my date. I haven't had that much fun dancing in a long while."

"I enjoyed myself. You ladies are something else. I didn't realize people still had the same relationship drama as in high school."

She laughed. "Tonight was mild compared to the reunion. And Darlene…," she shook her head, "that girl has been after Byron since high school. He didn't pay her attention then and he certainly won't start now. He and Nzinga were meant for each other, and I'm so glad they were finally able to be together."

"I agree. They make a nice couple and seem happy." Chris contemplated her statement. The notion of being meant for someone had never crossed his mind, even with the woman he married. They'd gotten along fine and he'd been in love with her, or what he thought was love at the time. However, the emotions he felt whenever he was with Max let him know he hadn't had a clue about the true meaning of love back then. It had taken him over two years to fall in love with Janine and propose marriage. Over the past several weeks, he'd begun to analyze and compare the relationships and he realized that his and Janine's relationship was one of comfortability. He knew her, she knew him, and he didn't have to worry about the dating scene being in his mid-thirties. His feelings for Max far eclipsed those he'd had for his ex, and in a much shorter time frame. What he had with Max was special and he wanted to believe that things would work out this time. *The Davises don't do well in long-term relationships*, a nagging inner voice shouted. *Just look at your family tree.* Chris pressed a button on the stereo and music flowed through the speakers, drowning out the annoying thoughts.

"Aw, wait now. Is this Bootsy?"

Chris grinned. "Yes. It's from his most recent release and features George Benson."

Max whipped out her phone. "I'm behind on my music."

"What are you doing?"

"Getting ready to download the album." She glanced at the stereo's digital display, then back down at her phone. "The Power of the One," she mumbled. "Found it."

"I take it you're a music lover."

"You can't tell?" she asked with a chuckle.

"Well, the dancing and singing to every song might have given you away. If you love it so much, why didn't you play in the band like Val?"

Still nodding to the beat, Max said, "We did play together in junior high—me on the saxophone and her on the drums—but I found out I enjoyed playing sports more. By the time we got to high school, I'd left music behind completely."

"Can you still play?"

"Probably if it's "Mary Had a Little Lamb. What about you?"

Chris laughed. "Music was for entertainment only. Like you, I focused on sports." They spent the remainder of the drive home discussing the various sports they enjoyed. He parked in her driveway and went around to help her out of the car. As she stood, the slit fell open, giving him an unhurried view of her bare legs and making his arousal surge once again. He cradled her hand in his and escorted her to the door.

"Come on in," Max said tossing her purse on the sofa. "I had a fabulous time tonight."

"So did I." And he didn't want it to end. He shut and locked the door, then closed the distance between them. She looped her arms around his neck the same time as his arms went around her middle. He covered her mouth in a gentle kiss, infused with all the passion that had been steadily rising from the moment they'd met. His hands roamed down her back and over her hips, and he pulled her soft curves closer to the fit of his body. She moaned and the soft sound sent heat spiraling through him. At length, he eased back and rested his forehead against hers, both their breathing ragged. He closed his eyes briefly and tried to force air back into his lungs. "Max."

She placed a finger on his lips. "I think I'm ready to indulge in that decadent dessert, or maybe that something better you mentioned."

"Are you sure?" The words were music to his ears, but he didn't want either of them to have any regrets.

"I'm positive, Chris. I want this. I want *you*."

That's all he needed to hear. Chris swept her up in his arms. "Which way is your bedroom?"

She pointed. "End of the hall. Door on the right."

He strode in the direction she indicated and sent up a silent thank you that he'd remembered to purchase condoms.

CHAPTER 8

*M*ax's breath stacked up in her throat as Chris unzipped her dress and trailed his tongue down her spine. She felt as if she was coming out of her skin.

"This is another one of those other things that I haven't done in a while, so it might get a little wild before the night's over," Chris said while kissing her down onto the bed and slowly divesting her of her clothes.

Have. Mercy! If this was anything like his kisses, that hot night of sex she and Nzinga talked about might just become a reality, instead of a very sensual fantasy. His hands and mouth made her body come alive in a way it never had and she couldn't stop the moans spilling from her mouth.

His hand caressed her hip. "I've wanted to touch you like this since the first day I saw you lying on my floor in those black knit pants."

She recalled that day and smiled. "Is that the day you were in the kitchen drinking water?"

"You almost made me choke. I could barely breathe."

Max laughed softly. She had wondered about it and remembered how intensely he'd stared at her when she asked if he was okay. She'd felt the attraction even then. "I'm glad you didn't choke."

"Me, too. I would've missed all this. You are a beautiful woman, Max," he said almost reverently as he caressed her cheek. Chris eased off the bed and began to undress.

She couldn't take her eyes off him. She'd felt the strength in his body, but for a man about to hit the half century mark, he had a slender, muscular build of someone at least a decade and a half younger—tight and toned. Obviously, he put his home gym to good use. Max watched as he rolled the condom over his engorged shaft and a moment of panic hit her. It had been a good three years—or was it four—since she'd had sex. Then there was the whole menopause thing. Hell, she didn't even know if everything still worked.

"What's going on in that beautiful head of yours?" Chris asked, joining her on the bed again. He wrapped his arms around her and kissed her temple. "Are you having second thoughts? If you are, I'm good with us just lying here together. We don't have to do anything you aren't ready to do."

His statement earned him a whole pan of brownie points. "I'm not having second thoughts. It's just…it's been so long and being of a certain age, it could be as dry as paper down there. Maybe I should've bought some lubrication or some-thing. I don't want to be messing up my night after you've gotten my body all on fire."

He lifted his head, stared at her for a moment, then burst into laughter. "Max, you are a priceless jewel. Baby, our night won't be messed up, and I can promise you I have all the lubrication you'll need."

She blinked. "You—" That was the only word she managed before he captured her mouth with lightning speed, sending her senses spiraling out of control. His hand slid up her thigh and shock waves of desire hummed through her veins. She ran her hand over the hard planes of his broad chest and around to his nape.

"I can't get enough of kissing you," he murmured, transferring his kisses to her throat, while his hand came up to caress her breasts. He replaced his hand with his tongue, circling one taut nipple, then the other. "Max, sweet Max."

"Chris," she whispered, feeling as if she was coming out of her skin as he kissed his way down the front of her body. He left the bed briefly and reached for something she couldn't see, then returned. Max gasped softly when he parted her thighs and trailed his tongue along her inner thigh to her warm, moist center, then mirrored his actions on her right leg. He repeated the action until she trembled and writhed beneath him, then plunged his tongue inside her. Max screamed his name and gripped the back of his head, holding him in place. Chris made one long swipe across her clit and she cried out again. She felt something warm, then hot. Her hips flew off the bed. "What is that?" she asked breathlessly.

Chris glanced up at her briefly with a pleased male smile. "Just a little something I picked up from Desiree's shop."

Max had difficulty processing with her mind clouded in a sensual haze. Finally, it dawned on her. *The massage oil.* She fisted her hands in the sheets as his tongue delved in and out of her, the slow, hot licks and warm oil pushing her higher and higher until she convulsed in a shuddering climax that made her scream out his name. He slid two fingers inside and kept up the twin assaults and she came a second time.

He slid up her body and smiled down at her. "I think we'll be fine in the lubricant department."

She barely registered his words as she lay there pulsing everywhere. He didn't give her time to recover as the sensual pleasure began all over again.

He shifted his body over hers and eased inside her until he was buried to the hilt. He closed his eyes and groaned, a look of pure ecstasy on his face. "You feel so good, baby," he whispered against her lips, at the same time he started moving inside her.

"Mmm, and so do you." Max wrapped her legs around his waist and pulled his mouth down on hers, their tongues tangling and dancing. Their eyes held as he started a slow rhythm, pushing deep, withdrawing to the tip, repeating the action several times. What he was doing to her felt so good she didn't ever want him to stop. His strokes came faster and harder, and she cried out with pleasure. She met and matched his thrusts, their breathing growing heavier and echoing in the quiet space. Shivers of delight spread through her and she arched up higher, yearning for release. This time the sensations began low in her belly and flared out to every part of her body. And suddenly her body was shaking, and she came with a soul-shattering intensity. Max exploded with white-hot pleasure, shuddering uncontrollably and screaming out his name again. *"Chris!"* The sensations continued for what seemed like hours, then she felt him go rigid.

Chris tore his mouth from hers, threw his head back and let out a low growl. His body shuddered above hers, his breathing harsh and uneven.

He stared down at her for a long moment and Max's emotions swelled. This went way beyond sex. He used a finger to trace her lips and gazed at her with such tenderness, tears pooled in her eyes.

He lowered his head and kissed her tenderly. "Thank you." He withdrew and rolled to his side, taking her with him.

Max lay her head on his chest and smiled. She could answer her sister's question definitively—he did not suck in the bedroom. If he were any better, she might not have survived. As it stood, she was still trying to catch her breath.

Several minutes later, she said, "I am never believing anything you say again about being *rusty* or *out of practice*."

Chris chuckled. "I guess it's true what they say about once you learn, you never forget." He pulled her on top of him. "Are you ready to get wild?"

She raised an eyebrow. "Am I laying naked on top of you?" He reached for another condom and she snatched it and slowly rolled it over his rapidly growing erection, teasing it over his flesh as she went.

He gritted his teeth. "Woman, are you trying to torture me?"

"Just giving you a taste of your own medicine this time around." Finished, she lowered herself onto his erection, swiveling her hips in a figure eight. The moment their eyes connected, she knew she'd fallen for him. Completely.

"You're a hard man to catch up with these days," Matt said, sipping from a bottle of beer out on his deck Sunday afternoon. "And you missed the barbeque last weekend. There were at least three women who asked about you. I've never met anybody who would rather sit around in that big house of yours doing nothing than getting out and enjoy life. You're turning into a recluse, Chris, and that's not good."

Chris didn't reply immediately. His friend was right on one hand. He had been living a solitary life, only venturing out occasionally for socialization. That had changed since he'd started dating Max. He hadn't accepted social invitations from Matt or his few CHP buddies, but this time, it was for a completely different reason. "For your information, I wasn't sitting around my house. I had a date."

Matt choked on his drink and sat up abruptly, coughing and trying to clear his throat. He shot Chris a look. "A *date*?"

"Don't look so surprised. I do go out occasionally."

"More like rarely. So are you going to tell me about her or sit there and make me play twenty questions?"

"Her name is Max and we met a couple of months ago. She's…Malia's occupational therapist."

"Back up. Is this the new therapist you mentioned a few weeks back? The one who you said is doing well with your niece?"

Chris nodded. "She does very well with Malia. Sandra calls Max a baby whisperer." If he were being honest, he'd call her a man whisperer, as well, because she'd reeled him in so fast, he still didn't know what had hit him. The image of her riding him last night popped in his head, along with the profound pleasure they'd shared. He had felt as if she'd extracted part of his soul.

"Exactly how long have you been seeing Max?"

"A couple of months, give or take a week or two. I really like her," he said quietly.

"It's about damn time you found somebody else. The best way to get rid of bad memories is to replace them with some better ones." Matt lifted his bottle in a mock salute.

He didn't know about replacing the bad memories, but he and Max were certainly creating new ones. Ones he knew would be permanently etched in his brain.

"What does she look like?"

Chris smiled. "Absolutely gorgeous. She's about five-eight with enough voluptuous curves to cause a wreck." He recalled one man at the dance staring so hard at Max that he'd tripped over a chair.

Matt chuckled. "In other words, a grown-ass woman."

He touched his bottle against Matt's. "Definitely. She's direct and doesn't mince words, either." He shared the details of their first encounter, including him almost choking on his water. "I have never met a woman who could slice you so sweetly, you don't know you've been cut until you see the blood. And do it with a smile."

Matt exploded in laughter. "I would've given anything to see that. When it comes to you, all women tend to do is bat their eyelashes and trip over themselves to be at your beck and call. It's good to know there's finally a woman giving you a run for your money. I hope you don't plan on relegating her to your has-been list any time soon."

Chris shot Matt a glare, which his friend ignored.

"Don't cut your eyes at me. You know how you do."

"You act like I treat women bad, and I don't. I just let them know the rules up front." Except, everything that had governed his past relationships had gone right out the window when he met Max. Usually, he lost interest after a date or two, and none of the encounters included sex. But the more time he spent with Max, the more he wanted to know about the fascinating woman who'd given him a reason to hope again. The doubts still lingered in the back of his mind, but Chris had done a good job keeping his demons at bay, so far.

Matt snorted and waved a dismissive hand. "You and those damn rules. What you need to do is screw all that mess and just let yourself feel for once," he added pointedly. "There's nothing like loving and having the love of a beautiful woman. Not everyone is like Janine, bro."

Chris' jaw tightened. He'd tried over the past several years to purge Janine from his memory, and didn't like being reminded of her betrayal.

"Speaking of the witch, I ran into Don last week. He had the nerve to tell me he didn't understand why I was still mad after all these years, especially since it had nothing to do with me. I started to knock the hell out of him to remind him just why I'm still pissed." Donald Collins had been the third member of the trio of friends, but his treachery had effectively shattered the bond of friendship that had spanned almost three decades.

"Better you than me." He had run into Don a few years back and had walked away, rather than stand around to listen to whatever lies the man wanted to tell. Chris had said everything he needed the day Don had ruined what was supposed to be the happiest day of Chris' life. He tilted the bottle to his lips, drained the contents, then set it on the small table next to his chair.

"Yeah. Anyway, back to this new woman. Will we get to meet her before you cut her loose? You're at the two-month mark already, which means we've got what…another couple of weeks or so."

"I don't plan to cut her loose. She's different, Matt." He hadn't talked to Max since leaving her house early that morning, and he wanted to see her again, to take that trip back to ecstasy one more time. Chris had endured endless teasing over the past couple of years because of his decision to remain celibate. He was far past the age of jumping in and out of bed with any and every woman—he'd never done it—and he'd grown tired of the dating scene. He had lost count of the many blind dates and matchmaking schemes from his friends who thought they were "helping." What he'd come to realize recently was that he had been waiting for one woman. The right woman. Max. In her Chris had found everything he never thought possible in a relationship.

Matt leaned up and studied Chris. "You're in love with her." It was a statement, rather than a question.

He'd just realized the depths of his emotions and wasn't quite ready to share, so he simply said, "I don't know, but I really like her." He looked forward to their walks, the quiet times where they sat cuddled together and of course, the passion. What they shared hadn't merely been sex. They'd shared themselves, body and soul. They'd made love. *Love.*

The word usually had him cutting bait and running for the hills, but this time he didn't want to walk away. He couldn't walk away. And he'd finally figured out why—he was falling in love with Max. He, who had never believed love at first sight existed, had been proven wrong. If he were being honest with himself, he'd have to admit that he had probably fallen for her the moment she crossed the threshold of his home.

"I definitely need to meet this woman. And *soon*."

"We'll see. Then again, maybe I should bring her over. At least I'll know you and your matchmaking wife won't be trying to hook me up with one of her crazy friends."

Matt laughed. "Hey, we're just trying to get you blessed."

Chris grunted. "I'll stick to getting my own blessings, thank you." Without a doubt, he counted Max as a blessing sent from above. And he couldn't wait to show her just how much she'd enriched his life. He had made a practice of not being home during her therapy sessions because she tempted him in ways he couldn't describe However, this week, not only would he be there, he also planned to kiss her until he got his fill.

CHAPTER 9

$\mathcal{M}$ax placed a platter of fluffy waffles in the center of her dining room table and sat. She and her girls were originally scheduled to have lunch next Saturday. But when she and Chris were leaving the dance last night, Val had whispered that they planned to be at Max's house the next day to get all the details about Chris. Even though she was tired, she'd gotten up and made a Sunday brunch menu that included waffles, scrambled eggs, bacon, sausage, fruit and plenty of mimosas.

"Girl, those waffles look amazing," Donna said, reaching for one.

Nzinga followed suit. "I agree. I haven't had them in so long. I might have to make them next weekend sometime."

Max smiled. "I know Bryon will be happy." She added some of everything to her plate. "Y'all know I love you because I made the syrup."

Val paused in mid-pour. "Oh, no you didn't. When did you start making homemade syrup?"

"Since I found the recipe a few months ago. It's vanilla maple syrup and it's so good."

"Oh, my goodness. It is," Donna said, moaning. "Okay, Nzinga has the fried chicken and Max is the waffle and syrup queen. Val, you and I can just eat."

Val laughed. "I'm down with that." She lifted her cranberry mimosa. "To Max and the best damn syrup around." They all touched glasses.

"Amen." Nzinga forked up another bite. "Alright, Max, that Christian is fine, girl. Did you see all the heads turn when you two walked in the room?"

"Honey, those women snapped their heads around so fast, I'm surprised none of them ended up with whiplash," Donna said.

"I still can't believe that Darlene Butler tried to invite Byron and Chris to an *after party* with one of her girlfriends." Nzinga took a sip of her drink before continuing. "She'd better be glad I didn't hear it. And she was a little upset to find out that Byron and I were married."

"You and me, both. She knows damn well Byron was with you at the reunion," Max said. Darlene had always had a thing for Byron and it was clear the woman still didn't know how to take no for an answer. "Chris didn't say anything more about it after we left."

"Probably because he didn't think it was important," Val said. "The man only had eyes for you. Girl, if a man looked at me that way…" She shook her head.

Donna chuckled. "It was getting real hot at the table."

Max pointed her fork Donna's way. "Oh, and don't think I'm going to forget about you humming that song."

"What? I don't know what Chris whispered, but *everybody* could feel the heat between you two. I'm sure your evening ended with more of those 'out of practice' kisses." She made quote marks in the air.

"It ended with a lot more than that," Max mumbled.

The three women froze, then screamed, "*What?*"

Nzinga snapped her fingers. "That hot night of sex, huh?"

"*Blazing*," Max confirmed, fanning herself. Even now, the memory of their lovemaking sent heat spiraling through her. She didn't think she would ever forget his comment about the lubricant. The man had banished whatever apprehensions she'd had with one sensuous stroke of his tongue. "I'm just glad it hadn't dried up after not being used for so long."

The women howled with laughter, and Donna said, "Only you, Max."

"I'm just saying." She put her fork down. "He's so different in a good way. He makes me feel…I don't know."

Nzinga nodded. "I know what you mean."

"It's crazy. I've only known him for a couple of months, but I think I'm…I'm falling in love with him."

"Oh, Max, that's wonderful," Val said.

"Maybe, but don't you think it's too soon to feel this way? I've been out of the game for so long, I can't remember how this is supposed to work." Hearing herself say the words out loud gave her a moment of pause. She always talked a good game when it came to relationships and usually had no qualms about going after what she wanted. But this thing with Chris had grabbed her so quickly, she wasn't sure about anything.

"Sis, there's no timetable for falling in love." Donna shrugged. "It happens that way sometimes. As long as he doesn't hurt you, we're good. It's time for you to find a man who will treat you with the love and respect you deserve. If that's how you're feeling about Chris, then roll with it. Have you told Dion about him?"

"Yes. Chris called the day Dion came over." She snapped her fingers. "Oh, I didn't get a chance to tell you Rolando dropped by last Friday. It was him at the door, and not Chris, when we were on Zoom. He was mad because he thought I'd told Dion about his lies, but he got his ownself caught.

Apparently, when he got married, the minister mentioned he'd been waiting for them to tie the knot for seven years. Dion did the math and realized I'd been telling the truth. Now he won't talk to his father."

Nzinga shook her head in disgust. "So because he got busted, Rolando's trying to blame you. Dumb ass."

"Chris showed up and had to hold me back from kicking his ass. Do you know he had the nerve to call me out of my name?"

"Oh, *nooo*. I would've knocked him out."

"I did. Knocked the word *bitch* right out of his mouth. Out the door and down the steps. And told him he'd better not show up at my house again."

"What did Chris do?" Val asked.

"He told Rolando he would only get that one warning."

Donna clapped. "That's what I'm talking about. A *real* man. I think he might be a keeper."

"I think so, too." Max could still recall how he'd held her so protectively in his arms.

"Have you two talked about where the relationship is headed?" Nzinga asked.

"No. I—" The ringing of her phone interrupted her reply. "Let me get that," she said, pushing back from the table and rushing over to the china cabinet where she'd left the cell. Her hand paused on the button and her pulse skipped when she saw Chris' name on the display. "Hello."

"Hey, baby. How's your day going?"

Every time he called her *baby*, it did something to her. The way he said it in that deep, melodious voice made her *feel* as if she really was his baby. And more. "It's going well. Right now, Nzinga, Val and Donna are here. We're having a late brunch." She lowered her voice to a whisper. "I'd planned to do it earlier, but somebody, who shall remain nameless, kept me up late last night."

Chris' low chuckle came through the line. "And I'd do it again. In a heartbeat. All I need you to do is say when."

Max closed her eyes to steady herself. It was on the tip of her tongue to blurt out the word *when*, but she remembered that she had company. She risked a quick glimpse over her shoulder and found all three of her friends smiling at her. She rolled her eyes and bit her lip to keep from smiling.

"Hi, Chris," they chorused in singsong, then burst out into a fit of giggles.

She whipped her head around and gasped, then skewered them with a look.

This time Chris outright laughed. "Byron was right. Y'all love to act up. You ladies are something else."

"Or something," she conceded. She couldn't even pretend to be mad at her girls because they'd done the same thing when Byron had called during one of their lunches.

"I'm not going to hold you. I just wanted to hear your voice. We can talk later. You're turning me inside out, woman," he added softly.

If she hadn't already been falling in love with him, his statement would have shoved her off the cliff. "Same. I'll talk to you later." Max disconnected the call to keep from blurting out that she loved him. She held the phone against her heart and waited for her emotions to regulate.

"You okay, Sis?"

She gave Nzinga a soft smile. "Yeah. I'm good." She was better than good.

Max parked in front of Chris' house. She was a little early, so she sat for a moment. Over the past month and a half, she'd fallen deeper in love with him, but had not yet told him. She wanted to believe he felt the same—everything he said and did indicated that was the case—but he hadn't mentioned it, either. He had yet to meet her family, although her mother had invited him to Thanksgiving dinner. Max wasn't upset he declined, because she knew spending time with his sister was important to him. But they'd spent most of every weekend together, and got together at least once or twice during the week.

It had gotten harder and harder to maintain the bounds of her professionalism when she came to his home each week. She sensed he understood because he, most often, didn't arrive until after she'd gone. But for some reason, today she wanted to see him, feel his strong arms around her. Releasing a deep sigh, she took the key out of the ignition and reached for the door handle. Her cell rang. She smiled and connected. "Hey, Gypsy." Even though her sister had moved back home, the nickname still stuck.

Teresa laughed. "Hey, girl. I know you're probably on your way to play with the babies, but I wanted to know when I'm going to get to meet Mr. Fine. Especially since I think he's going to be around for a *long* time."

"What makes you think that he'll be around?"

"Because I don't think I've ever seen you this happy with a man, what's-his-name, included. And because Chris gives you that good, makes-you-wanna-scream loving. I know you aren't crazy enough to walk away from that."

Max shook her head. *This girl.* "Teresa, you don't have one ounce of sense. I'm not the one who's crazy. I don't know when you'll meet him, and I'm hanging up."

"Bye," Teresa said, still cracking up.

"Little sisters," she mumbled, getting out of the car. After gathering her toys, she started up the walk. Max raised her hand to knock and the door opened, slightly startling her. "Hi, Sandra."

Sandra smiled and held the door open. "Hey, Max. Come on in," she whispered. "You have got to see this."

She followed the woman through the foyer to the living room and stopped short. Chris was stretched out on the floor with Malia lying on his chest—one hand wrapped protectively around her and the other folded beneath his head—and both were sound asleep. The sight made her heart melt. She carefully placed her duffle on the sofa and it took everything in her not to whip out her phone and snap a picture to capture the sweet moment.

Sandra motioned for Max to follow her through the kitchen to the family room. "We can talk in here for a few minutes before I wake the little missy. She's really coming along. I know there haven't been any huge gains, but every small success is a celebration to me."

"As they should be. Do you have any questions about the activities, or any concerns?"

She shook her head. "I did want to talk to you about something, though."

Somehow, Max already knew what the younger woman wanted to discuss. "Okay," she said slowly.

"I wanted to thank you. My brother has never been this happy, and I know it's because of you."

"Sandra—"

Sandra held up a hand. "Please, let me finish. I know this is kind of awkward with me being the client and all, but I just wanted to give you some insight to why I want Chris to finally find love. I don't know what he's told you about our family—probably not much because he keeps things to himself mostly—but our parents were toxic, my father especially. He was an alcoholic and abusive. They argued and fought constantly, but my brother always made sure I was safe. After our father was killed in a drunk-driving accident, I thought things would get better. I was only ten years old, but I found out quickly my mother didn't want to be bothered raising another child. Chris is thirteen years older and had been more of a father figure to me than my actual father ever was, and I will always be grateful."

Max's heart broke listening to her story. Chris had mentioned the accident, but he hadn't shared the history of abuse. She didn't take offense because most men tended to be close-mouthed about their hurts. However, she did hope that he would one day feel comfortable enough to talk to her about it.

"He wanted to go into the military, but changed his mind because of me and went to college and got a degree in criminal justice, instead." Sandra paused, seemingly trying to control her emotions. "Chris is the one who helped me with my homework, took me to get my driver's license, went shopping with me to find my homecoming and prom dresses. And he's the one who cheered the loudest when I graduated from high school." A soft smile curved her lips. "If it wasn't for him, I wouldn't have gone to college. He paid for it all. My mother decided me enrolling in the university would be a waste of time, since all I should be concerned with was finding a good husband," Sandra said bitterly.

"I hear everything you're saying, but why are you telling me this?" The conversation had gone so far beyond professionalism that Max began to feel slightly uncomfortable. And she worried what Chris would say if he found out his sister was telling all his business.

"I just wanted you to understand how much he's sacrificed and how much I want him to finally experience what it means to find true love."

Had he not been in love with his first wife?

As if reading Max's mind, Sandra waved a hand. "I don't mean that first bit—. Um...I mean that other woman. Has he told you about her?"

"He mentioned what happened briefly."

Her hazel eyes, ones so much like her brother's, went cold. "She humiliated and hurt my brother, so I did the same to her. It's bad when you have to walk through your own reception to tell everybody your five-minute marriage is over because you got caught screwing the best man, but it's worse when you have to do it with two black eyes and a busted lip. Chris couldn't hit her, but I didn't have a problem doing it. I couldn't stand her trifling ass anyway, always batting her eyes and flirting with every man who crossed her path."

Before Max could stop it, a short bark of laughter bubbled up and escaped. "I'm glad you were there for him." She guessed Sandra felt it was time to have her brother's back the way he'd had hers all those years. She shook her head and checked her watch. They'd been talking for almost ten minutes and she'd had enough "Family 101" for one day. "I'd better get to work." They stood and went back into the living room.

"Well look who's awake." Sandra squatted down and picked up her daughter, who seemed to be quite comfortable lying on her uncle's chest.

Chris, who had still been asleep, came awake immediately, reaching for the baby.

Sandra chuckled. "Wake up, sleepyhead. You're blocking the therapy room."

He sat up and dragged a hand down his face. "Is it time already?"

"More like ten minutes past. Max and I were talking in the family room."

Chris finally noticed Max off to the side and came to his feet swiftly. "Max. Hey."

He gave her the smile that never failed to heat her up, and

she had to resist the sensual pull that made her want to walk over and greet him with a kiss. "Hey."

His grin widened as if he'd read her thoughts. "I'll get out of your way."

Max did her best to ignore his sexy swagger as he left, but her traitorous eyes followed him until she couldn't see him any longer. She turned back and met Sandra's amused expression.

"I'm glad to know the feeling is mutual between you two. He loves you," Sandra said, passing the baby off to Max.

Rather than comment, she sat on the floor and focused on her planned activities. By the end of the session, Max was more than pleased with Malia's progress. The little one seemed to be more animated and eager to play and had actually attempted to reach for the toys several times. Max took a few moments to talk to Sandra, then packed up.

"Come on, baby."

She spun around and saw Chris. He stood there smiling with his hand extended. She placed her hand in his and allowed him to help her up.

Without a word, Chris picked up her bag, waited for her to say goodbye then walked Max out to her car.

Max opened the trunk and Chris placed it inside. Up to this point, he still hadn't said anything, but the intense look in his eyes made her wonder what was going through his mind. She smiled up at him. "Thanks for the help." With lightning speed, he crushed his mouth against hers, slipping his tongue inside when her lips parted on a startled gasp. The first thing that went through her head: *I'm standing in the middle of the street.* The second: *Damn, this man can kiss!* The latter one promptly overruled the first thought and she came up on tiptoe to meet him stroke for stroke. When he finally lifted his head, they both were breathing as if they'd just run a marathon.

He rested his forehead against hers. "You have no idea how hard it is to have you in my home and not be able to kiss you like I want, to hold you in my arms. I try to stay away while you're here, but this isn't working for me, sweetheart. I can't keep pretending you don't mean something to me."

Each word hit her square in the heart, and truthfully, she, too, had grown tired of pretending, and wanted nothing more than to publicly acknowledge how much he meant to *her*. "Then don't."

Chris eased back, searching her face. "What are you saying, Max?"

Max framed his handsome face with her hands. "I don't want you to stay away when I'm here. I want you to greet me like I mean something to you and hold me so I'll *know* how much I mean to you. And tonight, I'll show you just how much you've come to mean to me."

"Baby," he whispered, peppering her face with kisses. "Will two hours give you enough time to get home and unwind?"

"Yes." It would also give her time to prepare herself to tell him she loved him.

Chris forced himself to stay below the speed limit as he drove to Max's house. It probably wouldn't look good for him to be stopped, and definitely not by one of his fellow officers. When he pulled into her driveway, he realized his hands were shaking. Never had he been so anxious to get to a woman. Then again, he'd never met a woman quite like Maxine Richardson, and something told him he never would.

Max came to the door with the phone cradled against her ear. "Hey. Come in," she whispered.

He placed a quick kiss on her lips and followed her through the house to the kitchen.

"Yes, someone just got here," she said, rolling her eyes. She opened the refrigerator and pointed to a shelf with a variety of beverages and mouthed, "You want something to drink?" He shook his head and she went back to her conversation. "Why are you worried about who is at my house? You haven't volunteered any information about who's in yours."

Chris grinned at her exasperated expression.

"What?" She sighed. "Yes, it's the same man." Max reached for Chris' hand. "Sorry. My son has forgotten that I'm the parent, not him," she said into the phone. "Wait. You want to invite us to dinner? You're ordering something, right?" She shook her head and said to Chris, "Dion is inviting us to dinner. I have to warn you, his cooking skills are still questionable."

"*Really, Mom,*" Chris heard Dion yell through the phone.

Chris chuckled. "Tell him thank you for the invitation, and we'll be there."

Max nodded. "Okay, when? We're going to grandma and grandpa's house tomorrow, so it has to be later in the week. Is Friday a good day?" she asked Chris.

"That's fine." He guessed he was going to meet the entire family in one week.

"We'll see you on Friday at seven. Now bye, boy." A smile softened her mouth. "I love you, too." She disconnected and tossed the cell on the kitchen table. "I'm so sorry. Until two months ago, I couldn't get him to talk to me for more than a minute. Now, I can't get him off the phone."

Chris brought her into his embrace. "Relax, baby." He lowered his head and captured her lips, kissing her slowly and thoroughly, until her annoyance subsided and only passion remained. His plans for them to talk first retreated to the back of his mind as the kiss deepened and her hands slid under his shirt and touched his bare skin. A shudder passed through him. "Max. We should talk."

"I don't want to talk right now. Didn't you say something about kissing me and holding me? About me meaning something to you?"

"Mmm hmm," he murmured, still kissing her.

"Then show me. It's the action that counts, not words, Mr. CHP officer."

Chris swept her into his arms and strode to her bedroom. "I've got action, Miss Therapist." It took him less than a minute to have her naked. "How's that?"

Max lay back on the bed. "I'd be much better if you were naked, too."

"Not a problem." He stepped back and nearly ripped his clothes off. He loved how Max embraced her sexuality. She never hesitated to let him know what she liked and what she wanted. No other woman he'd been with spoke her mind the way Max did and it was one more reason in a growing list of why she fascinated him. They'd made love three times, and each encounter took him higher than the previous one. After donning a condom, he came back to the bed and dragged his body along hers. In the blink of an eye, Max arched, flipped him over and straddled him.

"It's my turn to show you how much you mean to me."

She didn't give him a chance to reply as she slid down his body, removed the condom and took him into her mouth. *Oh, shit!* He felt his stomach muscles contract beneath her hands and his legs shook. She swirled her tongue from base to tip and sucked him in deep, eliciting a guttural moan from deep in his throat. Chris thought he was going to lose his mind. His breathing increased and his muscles quivered with each up and down movement of her mouth. She continued to torture him with her hands and tongue until he thought he would explode. He felt a wet and warm sensation that increased as she stroked him from base to tip and jerked upright. "What are you doing?" he said, barely able to get the words out.

She held up a small bottle. "Payback."

Before the words were out of her mouth good, the warmth ignited into a raging inferno and his eyes damn near rolled to the back of his head. What she was doing felt so good and he was two seconds from exploding. Unable to take it any longer, he pulled her up and slid his tongue between her parted lips. Chris reversed their positions and captured a chocolate-tipped nipple between his lips. He laved and suckled first one, then the other while charting a path down the front of her body with his hand. He slid two fingers into her slick, wet heat until she was writhing and moaning beneath him.

"Chris, *now!*"

He quickly found and donned another condom and entered her with one deep thrust. Any plans to take it nice and slow vanished as he set a pace that rocked the bed. She locked her legs around him and her hands burned a path over his chest and back.

"Yes-s-s!"

He lifted her hips as he plunged deeper and faster. Her whimpers and cries of passion excited him and pushed him closer to the edge. Their breathing grew louder as he gripped her tighter and drove into her harder.

Max arched off the bed and screamed his name. "*Chris!*"

Her body shook and her inner muscles contracted, clamping around him like a vise. Without warning, his orgasm started somewhere around his feet and shot through him like a crack of lightning. He threw back his head and exploded in a rush of pleasure that tore a raw expletive from his throat. He closed his eyes and groaned her name as spasms racked his body. When his breathing returned somewhere near normal, he stared down at her and kissed her tenderly. "I love you, Max."

Her soft gasp pierced the silence and tears pooled in her eyes. "I love you, too."

Chris covered her mouth in a deep, passionate kiss, filling it with everything he felt inside him. A frisson of fear crept up his spine, and he prayed this wouldn't end like all his other relationships because he wanted forever with her.

"$\mathcal{A}$re you sure you're okay with meeting my friends before we go to your son's house?" Chris asked as he drove. Matt had called and invited Chris and Max out for drinks because they wanted to meet her.

Max patted his thigh. "Stop worrying. Yes, I'm sure. Besides, if I order something strong enough, I won't notice Dion's bad cooking as much."

He laughed softly. "Is he that bad?"

"I have no idea. He's never been one for being in the kitchen. I let him cook breakfast once and he burned the scrambled eggs and the toast." She shifted in her seat to face him. "Who burns *toast*? You put it in a toaster with numbers on it, so you don't burn it. You might want to think about ordering a couple of appetizers with that drink to be on the safe side," she added with a little chuckle. "Although, when he came over last time, he did help me with dinner, but with close supervision and it turned out okay."

"You're a cold mom. I'll take my chances. The fact that he offered shows he's trying to make amends."

"Yeah, that and he's just trying to get into my business."

"Do you think he has a problem with us being together?" Chris hoped not because he didn't want Max put in a position to have to choose between him and her son.

"No. It wouldn't matter if he did. I'm a grown-ass woman and I don't need his permission for anything I choose to do with my life."

He pulled into the parking lot and found a spot near the front of the restaurant. Resting his arm on the steering wheel, his gaze roamed lazily over her body in the snug jeans and sweater. "I completely agree. You're definitely a *grown-ass woman*."

Max stared. "Um…I think we need to get out of this car."

A slow grin curved his lips. "Or I can move the car to the back of the lot and we can…" He shrugged. "It's been a while since I've made out in a car, but I think I can get up to speed pretty quickly."

Her mouth fell open and her face tinted.

Chris laughed so hard, he had tears. "Did I embarrass you?"

"Not at all. Just more shocked at my thoughts. I was actually sitting here debating whether to take you up on your offer."

It was his turn to be shocked when arousal hit him hard and fast. And *his* mouth dropped.

She reached over and pushed his chin up. "Close your mouth. Haven't you figured out by now that I'm game for most things?" she asked with a giggle.

She never failed to surprise him with her adventurous spirit. "I think," he said slowly, "I need that drink right about now."

Max fell against the seat and burst out in laughter. "Mmm hmm, that's what I thought."

Chris got out, went around to her side of the car and

helped her. With her hand tucked in his, they were still chuckling as they made their way to the entrance. Inside, he scanned the bar area in search of his friends and spotted them at the same time as Matt stood and waved. He led Max over and made the introductions. "Matt and Leila, this is Max." That's as far as he got before Leila jumped up and hugged him and Max.

"Max, I'm so glad to finally meet you," Leila said.

Matt smiled. "It's nice to meet you, Max."

"Same here," Max said, shaking their hands.

Matt waved a server over. "We went ahead and ordered our drinks. Shouldn't take long to get yours."

Chris seated Max, then took the empty chair next to her. "What would you like to drink?"

"Crown Apple and ginger ale."

He smiled, recalling her comment about having a stronger drink. He needed the same after that exchange in the car. A server appeared a moment later and he gave their drink order.

Leila beamed. "Chris mentioned you're an occupational therapist, Max. How long have you worked in the field?"

"Over twenty years. How long have you two known Chris?"

Matt leaned forward. "We go way back to when he was short, had bucked teeth and stayed in my house eating my mama's desserts. The boy could inhale a dozen chocolate chip cookies in less than ten minutes."

"Like you didn't do the same, and in less time," Chris shot back.

"Hell yeah, I did. It was my house, and I would've had *two* dozen if you'd stopped showing up."

The server returned with the drinks. Leila waved a hand. "Alright, you two. We have to make a toast." Everyone lifted their glasses. "To love."

They all touched glasses and Chris glanced at Max out of the corner of his eye to see her reaction, but her friendly expression hadn't changed. They chatted about the cold weather and upcoming Christmas holiday, but Leila kept finding ways to turn the discussion back to his and Max's relationship. After a while, Chris became uncomfortable. He appreciated Matt trying to steer the conversation back to safer topics, but Matt was no match for his wife.

"Are there wedding bells in your future?" Leila asked, dividing her smiling gaze between Max and Chris.

Matt covered Leila's hand. "Baby, chill on the interrogation. If they have something to tell, they will. They've been dating less than three months. With the way you've been grilling them, I'm starting to believe you should've gone to law school instead of court reporting."

Grateful he didn't have to answer the question, Chris finished his drink. The mention of marriage conjured up images of what happened the last time he'd made that trip down the aisle and once again, his anxiety spiked. He could see himself with Max long-term, but he sometimes wasn't sure he'd be able to let go of all the baggage to make it happen.

"That has to be fascinating," Max said. "I'd probably be so caught up in listening to the cases that I would forget I'm supposed to be typing. Is every day pretty much the same?"

Leila let out a short bark of laughter. "With what goes on, I can totally see that. And no day is the same. I might go in one day and counsel is in a good mood and greets me with a 'have a good day.' Then on the next they're pissed with each other and take it out on the reporters. But I can't imagine doing anything else."

They spent the next several minutes talking about topics ranging from their favorite musical artists to bucket list vacations. Chris checked his watch. "We should probably get going. I don't want to be late for dinner." He recognized the gleam in Leila's eyes—the same one she always had when she thought she'd found him the perfect wife—and decided on a hasty exit before she could bring up the subject of marriage again. After a round of *hope to see you again and goodbyes*, he hustled Max out the door. Fortunately, they were already in Natomas and made it to her son's house in ten minutes.

"Do you know what he's cooking for dinner?" Chris asked as they approached the door.

"No. I was afraid to ask, but whatever it is, I hope it's good." Max pushed the small white button on the side of the door.

"Hey, you made it." Dion reached out, hugged his mother, then kissed her cheek. He stuck his hand out. "You must be Mr. Davis."

Chris shook the young man's hand. "I am. Nice to meet you, Dion." Dion was a masculine version of Max. He stood around the six-foot mark and had the same dark brown eyes and smile as his mother.

"Please come in." He led them into a spacious living room.

"So how long before we got here did you finish cleaning the place?" Max asked, scanning the area.

Dion grinned sheepishly. "Um...ten minutes," he mumbled.

She laughed and patted his cheek. "I guess some things never change." To Chris she said, "I always had to threaten him when it came to cleaning his room. I'd give him days to get it done and it never failed, the child didn't do it until five minutes before he wanted to go somewhere."

"Can you at least wait until *after* dinner before embarrassing me in front of people?"

Chris chuckled. "I think that's a trait of all mothers." The two men did a fist bump.

Max skewered them both with a glare. "Really, Chris. You just met him two minutes ago and you're siding with him?"

He held up his hands. "Hey, I'm not on anybody's side. I was merely stating a fact."

She rolled her eyes. "Mmm hmm. Whatever. I need to go to the bathroom before we eat.

Chris followed her departure with a smile.

"Have a seat," Dion said, gesturing to the sofa. "I haven't seen my mom smile this much in a long time. Then again, I was part of the reason why she hasn't." He looked over at Chris. "She told you what happened?"

"Yes."

"My father made me believe she messed up our family and I did her so wrong. The worst part is that the whole time I was treating her bad, she never once stopped calling or asking me if I needed something."

Chris could feel his anguish. "Dion, your mother understands that none of what happened is your fault, and she doesn't hold it against you." But Chris did hold it against her ex and he truly hoped the man heeded the warning.

"That's what she said, but I don't know how to make up for everything I've done to hurt her."

"You don't need to make up for anything. What happened in the past is just that—the past. The only thing you can do at this point is go forward. She's knows you love her. Just be the young man she raised you to be and everything will work out."

Dion angled his head. "You care about my mom a lot, don't you?"

"I love your mother." And he did. Completely. But he still had the nagging fear that it wouldn't last. Chris had invested his whole heart in the relationship, and he did not want to feel the same pain as he had the last time. He wouldn't be able to survive because the emotions he had for Max were stronger and deeper than any other woman with whom he'd been involved.

"Please don't hurt her. That's all I ask. She's been through enough."

"I won't."

"Okay, what are you two in here whispering about?"

They both spun around to find Max standing a few feet away, hands on her hips, dividing a speculative glance between him and Dion. "Just getting to know each other," Chris said.

"Yeah, that's all, Mom."

Chris shared a look with Dion, an understanding that their conversation would remain between them.

Dion hopped up. "Are you ready to eat? I made chicken enchiladas, Spanish rice and a salad."

She lifted a brow. "Enchiladas? Where did you get the recipe?"

"From you." He guided her into the dining room and Chris followed. "It's the one you wrote down for me when I was a teen and never used it. I figured now is as good a time as any to try it out."

"Usually, you don't guinea pig guests the first time, son," Max said, shaking her head, but unable to hide her smile. She allowed him to seat her, then she rubbed her hands together. "Okay, bring it on."

While Dion went to the kitchen, Chris rounded the table and sat opposite Max. "He's a good kid, and he loves you."

"I know. He still feels guilty and I've been trying to help him work through it."

He reached over and grasped her hand. "He'll be okay. It's just going to take him a little time."

She gave him a soft smile. "You're right."

Dion returned with the serving dishes of food and placed them on trivets in the center of the table. He went back for a bottle of sparkling lemonade, then took the end chair.

"It looks and smells good, baby boy."

"Thanks. I hope it at least comes close to yours. I wanted to make this meal because it's one of your favorites."

"Thank you." A light sheen of tears filled her eyes. Max cleared her throat. "Alright, let's give this a taste." She filled her plate, while Dion poured the lemonade into three glasses.

After they fixed their plates, Dion waited for Max to take the first bite. Chris could tell he was nervous.

Max nodded slowly and her smile widened. "You did good, Dion. It's delicious."

Chris could see the relief on Dion's face. The young man's anxiety brought to mind the many times Chris had gone out of his way to try to please his mother. However, unlike Max, the only response from Chris' mother had been criticism. After a while, he stopped trying and focused solely on making sure Sandra had the love neither of their parents gave them. Picking up his fork, he cut a portion of the enchilada covered in green sauce and cheese and brought it to his mouth. He chewed and found it tasted better than what he'd eaten in some restaurants. "Your mom is right. It's really good."

"Thanks. I don't know anybody who cooks better than my mom."

Max paused with her fork halfway to her mouth. "What do you want?"

Dion's brows knitted. "I don't know what you mean."

"Are you trying to butter me up for some reason?"

He snorted. "As if it would work."

Laughter rang out in the room and they went back to the meal while conversing about Chris' CHP career, and Dion's new mechanical engineering position and women woes. Chris enjoyed watching the interaction between Max and

Dion. After witnessing her breakdown and hearing the pain in her voice when talking about the years lost with her son because of her ex-husband, it warmed his heart to see mother and son forging a new, and seemingly stronger, relationship. It made him speculate on whether he and Sandra would ever experience the same with their own mother. Chris didn't hold out much hope, though. Rosemary Davis had never been the quintessential mother who hugged her children or kissed away their fears, and he didn't see her starting now, particularly since she'd suggested Sandra put Malia in foster care. He could count on one hand the number of times she'd seen her granddaughter. Each of those times had been initiated by him or Sandra and always at Rosemary's house. The woman had never stepped foot in Chris' house in the fifteen years he'd lived there, even though he'd invited her several times. Dion's voice drew him out of his thoughts.

"Can I get you guys something else?"

"No, thank you. Everything was good. Your mom doesn't have to worry about you starving."

Max toasted Dion with her glass. "This was so good. I'm looking forward to what you'll cook next time."

"That means a lot, Mom," Dion said softly. "I'll even throw in dessert next time. I've got your triple chocolate chip cookie recipe down to a science."

"That was the only time you volunteered to help in the kitchen. All the other times, I had to drag you in kicking and screaming," she added with a smile. "I'm looking forward to the next time."

"And I'm hoping you'll come, too, Mr. Davis."

"Call me Chris, and I'd like that." Chris could tell his answer pleased Max.

Dion declined their offer to help clean up and shortly after, Chris drove back to Max's house. Once there, he followed her to her family room and saw several bags, baskets, ribbons and other types of packaging. "What's all this for?"

"The mothers of my babies." Max dropped down on the sofa and removed her boots. "Every year, I put together a little pampering gift basket for them. It's challenging having a child with special needs and they don't always have time for themselves, so this is my way of encouraging them to take a few minutes of respite. You can't take care of anyone else if you're running on empty. That's why I make a point of getting massages, manicures and pedicures and taking my long candlelight baths every month."

"You are a remarkable woman, Max," he said, sitting beside her.

"Thanks. And you'd better not say anything to your sister. Now, what's going on with you?"

Chris frowned. "What are you talking about?"

"You seemed far away sometimes this evening. And I've been feeling like you're pulling away ever since saying those three little words."

He had done his best to keep his turmoil hidden, but apparently he hadn't done a good job. How had she read him so accurately?

"If I'm not who you want, you need to tell me, so we don't waste any more of our time."

"I never said I didn't want you, Max. I want you and I love you, and being with you isn't wasting my time."

"But?"

"There's no but." He ran an agitated hand over his head. "Relationships just don't tend to work out for me in the end," he finally said. "Women don't have a monopoly on broken hearts."

"I see." She studied him for a lengthy moment. "Chris, I love you, and I know how it feels to have the one person who's supposed to be your forever hurt you." She shifted closer and stroked his face. "I can't erase what she did, but I won't stand in the shadow of it, either."

His heart started pounding. "What are you saying?"

"I'm saying you have to decide whether you're ready to risk your heart without reservation." Max stood and walked into the kitchen.

Chris buried his head in his hands and her statement echoed in his head. She'd nailed his feelings. *Am I more afraid of loving her or losing her?* Byron's words rushed back to him: *If you care about Max, you need to do everything in your power to keep her. Don't let what happened in your past rob you of having the right woman in your life. Max is beautiful and special, and if you don't want her, I guarantee there will be a line of men ready to step in and take your place.* Chris could either let his fears control him, or he could surrender to the sweetest love he'd ever known. He chose the latter. Coming to his feet, he headed toward the kitchen. Max stood at the stove, turning on a tea kettle. He came up behind her, slid his arms around her waist and pulled her against him. He closed his eyes as the love he felt for this one woman rose up and nearly overwhelmed him. "I'm not letting you go, Max. I love you too much, baby. I'm in this for the duration." Chris turned her to face him and tilted her chin and locked his gaze on hers. He wanted her to see the truth in his words. "You could never stand in the shadow of another woman because you're in a class all by yourself. You're mine."

"I'm so glad to hear you say that because I didn't want to have to hurt you. How're you going to have me fall in love with you and you out here acting up?" she fussed.

He couldn't stop the laughter that poured out of him. "I'm sorry. I'll make it up to you sweetheart. And before you say it, it'll be better than good. I don't want to get myself back into that ditch again."

"Ooh, you were this close." Max put her index finger and thumb together. "But I'll cut you a little slack this time."

"I appreciate it." And he appreciated having her in his life. Chris lowered his head and kissed her, his tongue tasting every area of her mouth. He gathered her closer to the fit of his body and deepened the kiss. *Yeah, she's mine. Forever.*

CHAPTER 11

"*Y*ou sound so happy, Max. Chris is good for you," Val said.

Max stuck her earbuds in and rushed around her bedroom packing. "He really is. I still can't believe he has me packing for an overnighter with no warning, no nothing." Chris had woken her up that morning and asked her to go away with him, and wouldn't even give a hint as to where they were going. He would be there in an hour. It had been two weeks since the night in her kitchen when they'd solidified the relationship, and she was glad things turned out the way she'd hoped. Chris had been even more attentive and she felt things were back to normal.

"It's Saturday and a little spontaneity is good. Don't forget some of that sexy lingerie you bought when we went shopping last time. You need to rock his world, not that you haven't done it already. What are you guys going to do?"

"I have no idea. He wouldn't tell me anything, except to bring one dressy outfit." She held up a red dress in one hand and a black one in the other before going with the black.

Val sighed dramatically. "That's so romantic."

"Do you ever think you'll marry again?" Val had lost her fireman husband in the line of duty.

"I honestly don't know. Sometimes, I think yes, if I find someone who loves me the way Byron loves Nzinga or the way Chris loves you. Then there's this part of me that wonders if I'll ever be able to love another man like I did Brad or will I just compare every man to him."

"I know he'd want you to be happy."

"Yeah, he would. Anyway, this isn't about me. It's about you and that handsome man of yours. Have a great time and you know we'll be expecting details. I think it's my turn to host lunch next. Hmm…it might have to be a mid-week dinner because we aren't waiting for an entire week, especially since Christmas is only a week and a half away and everybody will be busy."

Chuckling, Max said, "Get off my phone, crazy woman. I'll talk to you when I get back." Not two minutes later, her phone rang again. *My phone never rings this much on a Saturday morning.* This time it was her mother. She tapped the bud in her ear. "Hey, Mom."

"Hey, honey. What are you doing?"

"Chris is picking me up in less than an hour to spend the weekend with him."

"Oh, that's nice. He is such a handsome man. And his smile…"

She shook her head with amusement. "Mom, am I going to have to tell Daddy you're out her ogling other men?" Max and Chris had finally made it over to her parents' house for dinner and her mother had liked Chris immediately and went on and on about how nice he was and him being a cutie.

She giggled like a schoolgirl. "Child, please. I'm not dead and I'm just looking. Your father ogles those half-dressed women on the television, so I can check out a nice-looking man every now and again. I was going to invite you two over for dinner tomorrow, but you have better plans. Does he make you happy, baby?"

"Yes. Very happy, Mom. I love him and he loves me."

"Then that's all that matters. I won't hold you. Tell him hello and you two have a good time."

"I will. Tell Dad hello." They spoke a moment longer, then ended the call.

With no other interruptions, Max was able to finish packing and be ready when Chris arrived at exactly ten.

"Good morning," she said when she opened the door.

"Morning, baby." Chris gave her a soft kiss. "Ready?"

"Yes." She reached down for her rolling tote and garment bag.

"I got it." He carried them out to his car and placed them in the trunk. After helping her in, he rounded the fender and slid in behind the wheel.

"You're still not going to tell me where we're going?"

"Nope, so sit back and relax." He started the engine and pulled off.

Max stared. "Okay, then can you tell me what we're doing?"

"No," he said with a chuckle. "You've never had a man plan a surprise weekend before?"

"No." Rolando hadn't planned anything remotely close to a weekend in their entire marriage. He barely made dinner reservations. *He didn't have any problems scheming and planning to cheat on me*, she thought sarcastically. She'd dated Chris for three months and he'd done far more in that short time. Deciding to go with the flow, Max did what he suggested. She sat back, closed her eyes and relaxed. She had no idea she'd fallen asleep until she heard Chris calling her name and felt him touching her shoulder.

"Time to wake up, sleepyhead."

Sitting up, she glanced around and tried to clear the cobwebs from her brain. "Where are we? Sorry I fell asleep on you."

"It's no problem. We're in Sonoma. I thought we'd do a wine and food-tasting first."

"Sounds like fun." They got out and she tightened her coat around her as she peered up at the sky. "I just hope the rain holds off for a while." The temperatures hovered in the mid-fifties.

"I checked the weather, and it's not supposed to rain until tonight, but we'll see."

Chris gave their name to the hostess and she led them over to an area where two other couples waited for the tour guide. The tour lasted an hour and afterward, the couples enjoyed four wines paired with shrimp scampi ravioli, honey Dijon glazed pork tenderloin, fried game hen with an apple slaw and petit filet. When they finished, Max hugged Chris. "This was fun. Can we do it again when it gets warmer?"

"Absolutely. We can come back any time you want, whether here or Napa. There are also a few up near El Dorado Hills."

"I can't wait," she said with a wide grin.

"The hotel is not too far from here. We'll have enough time to check in before it's time for the next thing on the list."

"I was going to ask what that next thing is, but it would be useless, huh?"

He shrugged. "Pretty much."

Max couldn't be mad because he'd obviously taken a lot of time to plan the getaway. But after being single for so long and being in control of everything in her life, it was going to take some time for her to let someone else handle the reins. He drove another four or five miles before stopping at a beautiful hotel with lush grounds that reminded her of a tropical paradise. The large suite was just as lovely, but she only had time for a quick walk-through.

Chris held her hand and escorted her across the grounds to the resort's spa. "Couples massage up next, followed by a facial, manicure and pedicure for you. Consider this part of your 'me time' ritual."

She stood there amazed that he'd remembered parts of her self-care routine. How she loved this man. Her emotions welled up and she struggled to keep the tears at bay. "Thank you for this. I love you."

"I love you more." He gestured. "Shall we?" A staff member handed them robes and slides, and directed them to the appropriate locker rooms to change. Once they were ready, the massage therapists led them to a treatment room with two tables.

"We'll step out for a moment while you lie face down," one of the women said.

As soon as the door closed behind them, Max said, "It's kind of dangerous for us to be left alone pretty much naked. With all the sexiness you're packing, I might be tempted to straddle you on that table."

"And if she hadn't said they'd be back in a minute, I would let you," he said with a wink. "Now behave."

Max folded her arms and gave him a mock pout, but got onto the table and covered herself with the sheet. "Party pooper." He just laughed and followed suit. The massage was so relaxing, Max nearly fell asleep. And by the time she finished the facial and mani-pedi, she felt like a new woman. "So, I'm thinking I might want to add this to the future activities list, as well."

"Sweetheart, I'll add anything you want on that list. Ready to head back to the room? We have dinner reservations here in half an hour. It might be cutting it close, but will that give you enough time to change?"

"Plenty."

The suite had two bathrooms and by the time she came out, Chris, in a pale gray suit, was standing next to a table set for two. "We're eating here?"

"Yes. We can have dinner at a restaurant tomorrow, but I wanted you all to myself tonight."

"I'm good either way."

"And with the way you look in that dress, I think I made the right decision. You take my breath away."

She could say the same thing about him. From the first date until now, each one had been carefully planned down to the letter and clearly with her satisfaction in mind. He set the bar high for any man who might come behind him. Her heart clenched with the thought of him not being in her life. In the short time they'd been together, he'd impacted her in ways she had yet to understand. She only knew that he took her to a place no other man could.

Chris smiled and held the chair out for her. Instead of taking his seat immediately, he walked a short distance and picked up a Bluetooth speaker. "How about a little music to set the mood?"

A moment later, the wail of a saxophone filled the room. "Jackeim Joyner. You thought of everything."

"I tried," he said, taking his seat.

The meal was delicious, but she only had eyes for him. Near the end of the meal, he got up and retrieved a gift bag that she hadn't noticed from the end table.

"I got you a little something," he said, reclaiming his seat.

"We still have a few days before Christmas. Why didn't you tell me we were exchanging gifts? I would've brought yours."

"This isn't your Christmas gift. Open it."

Max lifted a brow, but didn't comment. She removed the paper and a huge grin covered her face. "I can't believe it.

How did you find this? I've been looking for months." He'd bought her another Black Panther wallet exactly like the one she had.

"I can't give up my secrets."

She was out of her chair and around the table in a flash. "Thank you, thank you," she chanted as she bent to kiss him.

"You're welcome. I have one more thing for you."

"This isn't fair. I didn't bring you—" He pushed back his chair and dropped to one knee, and she stopped mid-sentence. She brought her hands to her mouth. *Oh. My. Goodness. Breathe, girl. In and out, in and out.* Chris opened the little black velvet box, revealing a princess-cut solitaire that had to be close to two carats, surrounded smaller diamonds. She needed oxygen. *Stat.*

He grasped her hand. "Max, I love everything about you— your sexy smile, infectious laughter, the sweet *and* naughty things you whisper in my ear, your amazing and giving heart. I love the way we fit so perfectly. I cherish every precious moment with you and I want to experience them over and over for the rest of our lives. Will you marry me?"

"*Yes!*" He removed the ring from the box and slipped it onto her finger. A perfect fit. He stood and Max launched herself at him.

He swept her up in his arms. "I love you with everything in me."

"I love you, too," she whispered through her happy tears. Their lips met in a kiss to seal their promise of forever.

One month later.

Max stood in one of the hotel's rooms with her sister, three friends and Sandra waiting to exchange vows with Chris. Neither she nor Chris had wanted a huge wedding, instead opting for an intimate gathering with their families and closest friends. Max had met his mother briefly and the encounter had been somewhat awkward, as the woman didn't seem interested in her son's life. They had invited her to the wedding as a courtesy, but she declined and it made her sad for Chris. She could only hope the woman would come around at some point.

"That dress is stunning on you, Max," Donna said.

Val, Nzinga and Teresa all chorused agreements.

"Thanks." The knee-length champagne-colored silk sheath skimmed her curves in the best way.

"My new brother-in-law's eyes are going to pop out of his head when he sees all that cleavage," Teresa said, wiggling her eyebrows. "And when are y'all going to let me in to the sassy sisterhood?"

Sandra, holding Malia, said, "Sassy sisterhood? There's a

sisterhood? I was just thinking about getting a discount on therapy." They all laughed.

Val hugged Teresa. "Sorry, baby girl, but you're going to have to get your own sisterhood."

Teresa folded her arms and pouted. "That's just wrong. I'm sassy." She did a little strut. "Sandra, they said we're not *seasoned* enough to roll with them. Hey, we should get our own sisterhood."

"Ooh, I'm down with that." Sandra and Teresa exchanged a high-five.

"We have to think of our own name." Teresa tapped her chin, as if thinking.

The women dissolved in a fit of laughter and Max said, "Girl, just stop."

"Alright ladies," Max's mother said, entering the room. "It's almost time to get this show on the road."

One by one, they hugged and kissed Max as they left until only Max and her mother remained.

Her mother grasped her hands. "You look beautiful, baby, and I'm so happy for you. Have I told you how proud I am of you?"

"Oh, Mom. Please don't make me cry. All my life I hoped to be strong like you, to love unconditionally the way you do and to be as beautiful as you are inside. Because of the woman you are, I became the woman I am and I thank you." Her voice cracked.

"Now who's making who cry?" her mother asked through her tears. "You've always been my joy. I'm so glad Chris came into your life. He's a fine young man and he promised your father and me that he would always love you and take care of you."

"When did all this happen?"

"He came by the house a couple of days ago. That he took the time to talk to us told me all I need to know about him. I just wish he'd come along first. I never did like that Rolando, with him always walking around thinking he was better than everyone else."

Max's mouth dropped. "Wait. What? Mom, why didn't you tell me all this before I married the man?"

She waved a hand. "It wasn't my place. Besides, I'd still be praying for grandchildren if I had. With your sister gallivanting all over the globe, Lord knows it wasn't going to happen with her."

Max shook her head in amazement. "I love you, Mom." It was the only thing she could say. Minutes later, her father and son came to collect her. She had been surprised when Dion asked if he could walk her down the aisle, saying it would be his privilege to give her away to such an honorable man. Dion had also told her he was looking forward to getting to know Chris and being part of their lives.

"Ready, angel?" he asked.

"I've been ready."

Dion kissed her cheek. "You look amazing, Mom. I hope Chris is ready," he added with a grin.

She tossed him a wink. "I hope so, too." As they escorted her down the aisle, she barely registered the smiling faces. She only had eyes for the man to whom she'd surrendered her heart. He smiled at her in the way that made his eyes sparkle, making her pulse skip. Once they reached Chris and the minister, Dion kissed her cheek and stepped back.

Her father followed suit and said, "Be happy, sweetheart. Chris is a good man and I'm proud to call him son."

"Thank you, Daddy." She turned and placed her hand in Chris' as the minister had them recite their vows. Fifteen minutes later, she heard the words she'd been waiting to hear since the day he proposed.

"I now pronounce you husband and wife. Chris, you may kiss your bride."

"I love you, Mrs. Davis."

"And I love you," Max said through her happy tears. Chris' head descended swiftly and he kissed her with a passion that stole her breath and made her lightheaded. "I must say you're all the way up to speed with these kisses now."

Chris chuckled. "I plan to show you all the things I'm up to speed with tonight."

"Can't wait for that." They shared a smile and left to take pictures in the garden. The late January temperatures had risen to an unseasonably high of seventy with plenty of sunshine. On the way back inside the hotel, Max grabbed Chris' hand and went in the opposite direction of the reception hall.

"Isn't the ballroom in the other direction? Where are we going?"

"You'll see," she said without breaking stride. She entered the hotel room where she had dressed and closed the door behind them. For a moment, she just stared at Chris. He was really her husband now and she looked forward to spending the rest of her life with him.

"Max?"

"You told me what happened at your last reception, and I figure the best way to get rid of those bad memories is to create new ones." She unzipped her dress, stepped out of it and carefully laid it across one of the chairs, leaving her clad in nothing more than matching black lace panties and bra, and her heels.

Chris blinked and shook his head as if trying to clear it. "What did you say? Wait a minute."

A sensual smile playing around the corner of her mouth, she slowly closed the distance between them and reached for his belt. "This time, the only man your wife will be making love with is *you*. Right here. Right now." She undid his belt and unzipped his trousers.

His hands clamped down on hers. "Max, we can't... There are people..." His voice trailed off as his breathing became labored.

She ran her hand up and down his engorged length. "Am I going to have to torture you, or are you going to surrender willingly?"

Chris stepped back and discarded his pants and boxer briefs in the blink of an eye. "I'm waving the white flag, baby."

"Glad to hear it."

He swept her off her feet, placed her on the desk and slid her panties down and off. "Are you going to be this outrageous when we're old and gray?"

She lifted an eyebrow. "What do you think?"

"I think I'm going to be in for the ride of my life," he murmured, trailing kisses along her throat.

He thrust deep inside her and she gasped sharply. "I think *I'm* going to be in for the ride of my life right now. And since there are people waiting, we're going to have to make it a quickie."

His smile met hers. "Then let's ride," Chris said as he set a driving rhythm.

Max gripped his shoulders, threw her head back and it was her turn to surrender. To joy, to passion, and to the sweetest love she'd ever known.

Be sure to pick up
Love's Sweet Kiss
(Sassy Seasoned Sisters Book 1)

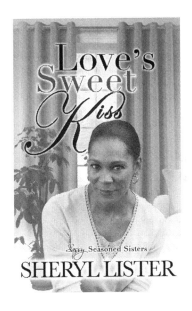

Nzinga Carlyle has finally gotten her life together after her divorce and is happily single. However, the moment she sees her teen crush at her high school reunion, old feelings start to rise. Nzinga isn't sure she's ready to move forward, although she can't deny the attraction between them. And after one sweet kiss, she has to decide how far she wants the relationship to go.

Byron Walker can't believe his good fortune when he runs into the woman who stole his teenage heart. Once he realizes their chemistry is still explosive, he vows not to let Nzinga get away a second time. Circumstances forced them apart over thirty years ago, but Byron intends to show her they were always meant to be.

EXCERPT FROM LOVE'S SWEET KISS

"I can't believe all the people who showed up for this picnic," Nzinga said as she, Val, Donna and Max entered their high school campus. The grassy area was filled with blankets, beach chairs and canopy shades.

"Maybe we should've gotten here a little earlier. I hope we can find a spot." Val pointed. "Look, there's an area over to the right."

The women quickened their steps to claim the spot and made it just before another group got there. They spread out the large quilt, raised the easy up shade and set up their beach chairs.

"I don't know why we needed to bring chairs, since we have the quilt," Donna said.

Max stretched her legs out. "Because I sit on the floor all week. Today, I want to be an adult and sit on a chair."

"Yeah, well, nobody told you to get a job playing with babies. If you wanted to be an adult, you should have chosen a different field."

"Shut up, Miss Rambo."

Donna smiled. "Damn straight."

Nzinga shook her head. These women filled her life with so much joy.

"Love the shirts!" a guy passing called out.

True to her word, Monique had designed gray tees with the words "Sassy Seasoned Sisters" written in a fancy font. She'd also added rhinestones because, according to her, they needed a little bling.

"Well, if it isn't the four Musketeers."

They all stood to greet Lamont Johnson, the jazz band's keyboardist and leader.

"Y'all haven't aged a day in thirty-five years."

"Please," Nzinga said. "It's too early in the day for lying." He'd added a good fifty pounds to his former string bean frame, but his smile and easygoing manner hadn't changed.

"I came to get my girl. We're going to start the music in about thirty minutes."

Val retrieved her drumsticks from her bag and held them up. "I'm ready."

"You know Desmond's here, and when he heard the band was playing, he had the nerve to ask could he sit in as drummer."

Max folded her arms. "And when you told him Val was playing?"

Lamont laughed. "Stomped off just like he did the first time. I'll see you over there in a minute, Val. Good seeing you ladies."

"Same here," they chorused.

Because of where they were seated, they had a good view of the mock stage. Confident that their belongings would be safe, the four women slung their purses on their shoulders and went over to get something to drink.

"I should've known she'd be one of the first persons we'd see today," Max grumbled.

Nzinga glance up to see Cassandra Butler headed their

way with the same stuck-up crew she'd hung out with in high school. Cassandra had never liked her and Nzinga had no idea why. But she figured that was a long time ago and water under the bridge.

"Hey, Valina, Maxine and Donna," Cassandra said as soon as she approached. She looked Nzinga up and down with disdain. "I see y'all are still hanging out with trash."

Nzinga had been determined to take the high road, but this heifer was going to make her lose all sense of decorum. She gave Cassandra a false smile. "I see you still are trash."

The two women with Cassandra nearly choked on their drinks. Cassandra took a step.

She lifted a brow. *I know she's not.*

Cassandra opened her mouth, then closed it and stormed off, her two minions following.

"I'm glad she decided not to cause a scene," Val said. "Maybe she's grown up some."

Max shook her head. "Nah, sis, that was a business decision. She remembered what happened the last time she tried to get in Nzinga's face."

Donna smiled. "Yeah, girl. She might still think she's all that, but she's not stupid."

Nzinga didn't care about the reason, she just hoped the woman kept her distance for the remainder of the weekend. In their freshman year of high school, Cassandra had made a habit of harassing Nzinga almost daily for a week. Nzinga grew tired of trying to be tactful and the next time Cassandra walked up, intending to start trouble, Nzinga dropped her with one punch, then walked away. "I'm not going to spend my time thinking about that crazy woman. We came here to enjoy ourselves, so let's do it." After getting bottles of tea, she, Donna and Max headed back to their spot, while Val went to join the band.

The band took them back, playing everything from

smooth jazz, to the R&B songs that had been popular during that time—"Cutie Pie" by One Way, "Forget Me Nots" by Patrice Rushen and "Take Your Time" by The S.O.S. Band—and had everyone on their feet dancing.

"Desmond doesn't look too happy," Donna said with a little laugh, pointing to where he stood near the stage glaring, no doubt, at Val as she flipped her sticks and never missed a beat.

Nzinga playfully bumped her shoulder. "I wouldn't either, if a *girl* could wipe the floor with me on the drums."

They launched into Earth, Wind and Fire's Shining Star and Max threw her hands in the air. "*Yaassss*! This is my *jam!*"

Apparently, that feeling was shared by everyone gathered —young and old—if the sheer volume of shouts that went up were any indication. At the end of the song, the audience all joined in to sing the final refrain acapella.

Nzinga clapped along with the crowd when it was over. "Oh, my goodness. They were fabulous. I didn't realize Val had kept up with her playing."

"Neither did I," Max said. "Girlfriend needs to put her pumps to the side and take this show on the road."

"No lie."

Donna elbowed Nzinga. "Girl, look who's coming this way."

She turned in the direction Donna gestured and saw Wesley Walker approaching with a man who she would recognize anywhere. Her heart started pounding just like it did the first time she'd seen him at their house when she and Wesley were working on a biology project. Byron stood six feet, four inches, had smooth, dark caramel skin and muscles for days. But it was his light brown eyes that had totally captivated her. And every other girl at the school. The way he stared at her now still had her mesmerized.

Max scooted close to her and whispered, "Honey, that

man is even finer than he was then. I sure hope he's single, especially since he can't seem to take his eyes off you. And that salt and pepper beard...*sexy!*" She cleared her throat and opened her arms. "Wesley Walker, the smartest guy in the world. How are you?"

Wesley laughed and embraced Max. "I don't know about that, but I'm good." He repeated the gesture with the other women, including Val, who'd just joined them. Then he placed his arm around a woman. "This is my beautiful wife, Loren."

Loren smiled easily and reached out to shake each of their hands. "I've heard a lot about you all over the years."

They all greeted Loren and Nzinga said, "I hope nothing bad."

"Not about you ladies, but I have heard a few stories about some others," she said conspiratorially.

Wesley chuckled. "Don't get her started." He introduced his two children. "I don't know if you all remember my brother, Byron. Lucky him, he came up for a visit just in time to attend this shindig."

"Who could forget the varsity basketball captain who led our team to the first championship in over a decade?" Donna said.

Byron smiled. "It's nice to see you ladies again." He turned to Nzinga and grasped her hand. "It's been a long time, Nzinga."

"Yes, it has." She ignored the knowing looks on her friends' faces. Nzinga thought herself far past the age of being affected by a man. But the mere touch of Byron's hand on hers made her pulse skip and had her heart beating at a pace that had to be dangerous. She couldn't remember the last time any man made her feel this way.

DEAR READER

Dear Reader ~

Whew! This installment of the Sassy Seasoned Sisters has been a long time coming. 2020 derailed my plans in a big way, but Max is finally here. And she's still as outspoken as ever. Christian definitely won't know what hit him and I hope you enjoy the sparks!

Love & Blessings!
Sheryl

sheryllister@gmail.com
www.sheryllister.com

ABOUT THE AUTHOR

Sheryl Lister is a multi-award-winning author and has enjoyed reading and writing for as long as she can remember. She is a former pediatric occupational therapist with over twenty years of experience, and resides in California. Sheryl is a wife, mother of three daughters and a son-in-love, and grandmother to two special little boys. When she's not writing, Sheryl can be found on a date with her husband or in the kitchen creating appetizers. For more information, visit her website at www.sheryllister.com.

.

Love's Sweet Kiss (Sassy Seasoned Sisters #1)

Never Letting Go (Carnivale Chronicles)

Embracing Ever After (Once Upon a Baby #1)

Do Me (Irresistible Husband)

Five Midnight Moments (New Year Bae-Solutions)

Tempting Hunter (Once Upon A Funeral #4)

Made in the USA
Columbia, SC
15 June 2021